"Come on, Jenna, it's singles night at Fred's Foodtown. It'll be fun. We can pretend we don't know each other," J.J. suggested.

"Don't tempt me."

"Maybe we'll bump into each other at the meat counter. I'll be eyeing your rump roast while you gaze raptly at my tenderloins."

"You're nuts, you know," Genna said evenly.

"Maybe we could squeeze each other's Charmin."

Genna couldn't help it. She started to giggle, then laugh outright. "Don't make me laugh," she said with a breathless gasp.

"Why not?"

"Because I'm liable to forget I don't like you."

"Would that be so bad?" he asked.

Genna sighed. "You're not what I need, J.J."

He pulled off her oven mitt and began caressing her cheek with it. "What about what you want?"

He was standing too close for comfort.

WHAT ARE *LOVESWEPT* ROMANCES?

They are stories of true romance and touching emotion. We believe those two very important ingredients are constants in our highly sensual and very believable stories in the *LOVESWEPT* line. Our goal is to give you, the reader, stories of consistently high quality that may sometimes make you laugh, sometimes make you cry, but are always fresh and creative and contain many delightful surprises within their pages.

Most romance fans read an enormous number of books. Those they truly love, they keep. Others may be traded with friends and soon forgotten. We hope that each *LOVESWEPT* romance will be a treasure—a "keeper." We will always try to publish

LOVE STORIES YOU'LL NEVER FORGET
BY AUTHORS YOU'LL ALWAYS REMEMBER

The Editors

LOVESWEPT® • 253

Tami Hoag

The Trouble With J.J.

BANTAM BOOKS
TORONTO • NEW YORK • LONDON • SYDNEY • AUCKLAND

THE TROUBLE WITH J.J.
A Bantam Book / May 1988

LOVESWEPT® and the wave device are registered trademarks of Bantam Books. Registered in U.S. Patent and Trademark Office and elsewhere.

ISBN 0-553-21900-6

Published simultaneously in the United States and Canada

Bantam Books are published by Bantam Books, a division of Bantam Doubleday Dell Publishing Group, Inc. Its trademark, consisting of the words "Bantam Books" and the portrayal of a rooster, is Registered in U.S. Patent and Trademark Office and in other countries. Marca Registrada. Bantam Books, 666 Fifth Avenue, New York, New York 10103.

PRINTED IN THE UNITED STATES OF AMERICA

O 0 9 8 7 6 5 4 3 2 1

One

Home. No four-letter word had ever sounded better, Genna Hastings thought as she maneuvered herself, careful of her sprained ankle, and her crutches out of her car. She stood up and took a deep breath of hyacinth-scented Connecticut air. Whack! Something hit her smack in the back of the head with the force of a Titan missile. Rubbing her head with one hand, she turned and stared down at the football that rocked harmlessly on the driveway beside her loafer-clad feet.

It was an appropriate ending to a thoroughly miserable vacation.

"Look out, Miss Hastings!" came the belated shout of one of the two boys pounding up the street toward her.

"Jeez, Miss Hastings, I'm sorry," said Brad Murray, stooping to scoop up the ball.

"Yeah, sorry, Genna," Kyle Dennison chimed in. Kyle was the chubby ten-year-old son of Genna's best friend, and so he felt entitled to call her by her first name. To Brad, she would always be his ex-kindergarten teacher. He would call her Miss Hastings for the rest of his life.

Kyle shrugged. "We didn't see you."

"That's a comfort," Genna grumbled to herself, wincing as she felt the goose egg rising on the back of her skull.

"Mom said you weren't coming home till Monday, and it's only Friday. Why aren't you still on vacation?

We've been using your driveway for long-passing patterns. Hey, how come you're on crutches?"

"All that in one breath," Genna said with a teasing smile as she looked down at Kyle. "Vacation was a bust. I sprained my ankle playing tennis."

"Bummer."

"Really."

"We're waiting for J.J." Brad said.

"Who's J.J.? New kid on the block?"

"J. J. Hennessy," they said in unison, staring at her expectantly.

Genna stared back at them. Was she missing the punch line of a joke, or what? "Am I supposed to gasp here, or scream or something? Who's J. J. Hennessy?"

The boys made sounds of disgust and rolled their eyes. Kyle collapsed onto the driveway and writhed around, holding his head.

"He's only the most awesome quarterback in the universe!" Brad raved.

"He's *so* excellent!" Kyle exclaimed, lying spread-eagled, flat on his back.

"And he's moved in right here!"

Genna looked at the lawn and house adjacent to the property she rented and felt suddenly as if someone had punched her in the stomach. The yard she had so admired had been cut in diagonal stripes. A dozen pink plastic flamingos lurked in the shrubbery, their long, craning necks poking up through boxwood and around juniper. Sitting in a lawn chair on the front porch of the lovely Federal-style house was a busty blond mannequin dressed in shorts and a tight pink T-shirt, one arm raised as if waving.

Genna sucked in a horrified breath. "Oh, my Lord."

"Cool, huh?" Brad said, mistaking her shock for awe.

Kyle struggled to his feet, nodding enthusiastically and tugging his T-shirt down over his pudgy tummy. "The mannequin's named Candy. Outrageous!"

"Oh, my Lord," Genna muttered again. What sort of

cretin would commit such atrocities? she wondered. That house and yard were the epitome, the essence of Tory Hills. Quietly lovely, old, and treasured. Occupying a large lot in the middle of the treelined block, the house was painted a sedate shade of gray, with white trim around the multipaned windows. The front entrance boasted a pillared portico and a graceful fanlight over the door. It was Genna's dream house. Now some tasteless moron had bought it.

The front door of the house swung open and Brad and Kyle went into a trance. They stared transfixed, as if they were awaiting a holy vision. Then J. J. Hennessy made his appearance.

Genna took one look at the man and despised him.

He swaggered across the lawn radiating arrogance like a furnace blasts heat. Over six feet of rippling muscle packaged in gray sweatpants that left nothing to the imagination but lewd fantasies, and wearing a torn black T-shirt that proclaimed him to be "God's Gift to Women," J. J. Hennessy appeared to be every inch the cocky, overbearing, aggressive male.

His black hair was sheared off on top in a spiky, grown-out crew cut but trailed down his thick neck in back. Square black sunglasses hid his eyes. His nose was short and straight. The idea of a smile played around the corners of his mouth.

Genna stared, aghast, as he sauntered across his striped lawn directly toward her. He stopped no more than two feet in front of her, hands on lean hips, a diamond stud glittering in his left earlobe. Then he looked down at her and smiled, and Genna actually felt her knees turn to cottage cheese. Unbelievable, she thought. He was everything she loathed in a man, yet she was trembling in the face of his charisma like some lovestruck teenager just because he had the most wicked Jack Nicholson grin since . . . well, since Jack Nicholson.

"Hey, J.J.!" the boys greeted him.

"Hey, guys, who's your gorgeous friend?" His voice was warm and rough, like corduroy. He could have read the Yellow Pages and sounded sexy.

I'm going to faint, she thought as that incredible voice washed over her. *Don't be an ass, Genna. He's a no-neck, boneheaded athlete who pillaged your dream house and thinks he's God's gift to women. Besides, you never faint.*

"It's just Genna," Kyle explained with no enthusiasm. "She lives here." He swung an arm in the direction of Genna's blue Cape Cod house.

"Well, well." J. J. Hennessy smiled once more. "Hel-lo, neighbor."

A pained smile forced up the corners of her mouth.

"Jared Hennessy." He captured one of her hands and managed to make a simple handshake seem lascivious. "Where were you when I was moving in? I could have used a hand with the decorating."

"So I see," she replied blandly, extricating her hand from his and absently brushing her tingling palm down the leg of her shorts. "I'm Genna Hastings. I've been on vacation."

"Did you have a nice time?"

"No."

"Have anything to do with those crutches?"

She gave him a smile that made her look as if she had a lip full of novocaine. "How very clever you are, Mr. Hennessy. I sprained my ankle playing tennis."

Jared dropped to his knees and started feeling the ankle she was keeping her weight off. For an instant Genna thought she was going into cardiac arrest. Lightning bolts sizzled through her veins. She couldn't breathe. Then she realized, with no small amount of astonishment, it was only her body reacting to J. J. Hennessy's touch as his one hand gently squeezed her ankle and the other wandered unnecessarily up and down her bare calf.

This is absurd, she told herself even as she began to get light-headed. He was the last man on earth she should be attracted to. She decided she would give him a scathing remark and jerk her foot away from him, but she found she could do nothing more than stare down at him with her mouth gaping open.

Jared grinned up at her. "Feels pretty good to me." His eyebrows bobbed up above his sunglasses insinuatingly. "Alternating hot and cold packs—that's the way to go."

"Thank you, Dr. Kildare," she said dryly, finally managing to step back.

"You're more than welcome to use my Jacuzzi," he offered, standing and backing Genna into the side of her car. He shoved his sunglasses atop his spiky-haired head.

Genna gulped. *Now you're really in trouble, Hastings.* His eyes were the most beautiful translucent blue she'd ever seen. Mesmerizing. Predatory. Like a wolf's, she thought. But there was a sparkle in them of . . . humor? It didn't quite fit with the bad impression she had formed of him.

Suddenly feeling off balance, she leaned back against her car. He stepped closer, resting one hand on the roof of the auto, inches from Genna's shoulder. She felt sweat break out between her breasts as a chill ran up her back. His gaze meandered down her body, seemingly burning off her yellow oxford-cloth shirt and khaki shorts as it went.

"How about it, Genna?" His voice had dropped to a velvety rumble. "I'd love to have you in my Jacuzzi." He drew his tongue across his lips and leaned closer, until he was no more than a thought away from pressing his body against hers.

Genna drew a shallow, shuddering breath.

"Come on, J.J.!" the boys' plaintive voices intruded. "Throw us a pass, will you? Pleeease!"

"Sure, guys." He turned, grinning, and accepted the football, his hands stroking it lovingly. "This'll be a long one, fellas. Brad, zig out left then cross back. Kyle, go straight."

With a quick motion of his arm, he fired the thing a good fifty yards down the block. The boys dashed after it like eager retrievers.

Jared turned back, his sexiest grin firmly in place, only to find his quarry had ditched him. The side screen door of Genna Hastings' little house banged shut, signaling her successful retreat. He smiled to himself. What a doll! She wasn't tall and svelte with a cover girl face like the models he'd dated in the past, but she was damn-darn adorable, from her twenties-style haircut right down to her preppy penny loafers. And to think he was going to be living right next door to that cute little curvy brunette. He chuckled to himself. "You lucky dog, Hennessy."

His life in Tory Hills wasn't going to be dull with Genna Hastings for a neighbor. Not only was she cute, she had *it.* The intangible factor, the odds makers called it. Jared just called it *it.* A fire, spark, an inner spirit. Genna had *it*, he could tell; he had a nose for that kind of thing.

Smiling, he closed his eyes and recalled her flashing smoke-blue eyes, tilted-up nose, and pained smile. Pained smile? He frowned. He'd have to work on that. All he needed was a little inside information, then he could come up with a game plan. She'd be smiling sincerely at him in no time. Confidence was seldom a scarce commodity for Jared Jay Hennessy.

He knocked his sunglasses into place and sauntered back into his yard, humming.

Genna sorted through her mail, still a little unsteady from her encounter with her new neighbor. Anger, she told herself. That was what was making her shake all over. Now that she was out of range of his sexy smile and bone-melting blue eyes, she could say that.

"Colossal jerk. He's a Philistine. A philandering Philistine who put flamingos in front of your dream house. Get that through your thick head, Genna Hastings!"

Memory of that gleam of humor in his eyes came back to her and threatened to soften her up, but she got a firm hold on those feelings and strangled them.

"God's gift to women," she muttered, tossing bills into one pile and personal stuff into another on the cherry dining room table she had rescued from a yard sale in the Berkshires.

"I'd love to have you in my Jacuzzi, Genna," she jeered, ignoring the fact that her leg still tingled from his touch. That sensation was obviously from the swelling. A couple of aspirins and an ice pack would take care of it.

Her heart did a little jitterbug as she recalled the hot look in his eyes just before the boys had called him off. She scowled. "Conceited creep."

A letter from her friend Mary Woods caught her eye as she tossed it onto the pile. It was postmarked Crested Butte, Montana. Montana? Mary had never been west of New York City. She tore the envelope open and extracted the note.

Dear Genna,

I met the man of my dreams at the corner of Park and Prospect. My car is a total loss, so is my heart. We've eloped! He's a rancher. Will send pics later.

Closed the catering service. Had to give all my business to Betsy—yuk! Sorry about the short notice. Hope you can find another summer job.

Gotta go. Matt's getting anxious to ride off into the sunset. I'll write again soon.

Love,
Mary

" 'Love, Mary'! I'll strangle her!"

"Strangle who?"

Genna didn't have to look up to know it was Amy Dennison letting herself in the kitchen door. Amy's distinctive if grating voice always gave her away. She sounded like a Volkswagen horn with a Brooklyn accent.

"Mary!" Genna remained seated at the table, glaring at the letter. "Do you know what she's done? She's run off with John Wayne and left me unemployed with a brand new car to pay for!"

Amy helped herself to a Coke from the refrigerator and plunked her chunky frame down on a Windsor chair opposite her friend. "Yeah, I'm happy for her too."

"Oh," Genna scowled, tossing the note aside. "Of course I'm happy for her, but I'd love to beat her with my bankbook! I was counting on that money when I bought my car. What do I do now?"

"You'll find something else," Amy said matter-of-factly.

"Sure," Genna said, her spirits sinking. "You know as well as I do that all the summer jobs are taken by the end of March."

Amy was silent for a moment as she stared out the window, her eyes fixed on the striped lawn next door, the kernel of a harebrained scheme forming in her mind. "Oh . . . I'll bet something will turn up."

Genna was too busy feeling sorry for herself to notice the odd note of excitement in Amy's voice. Here she was, just back from her disastrous vacation, with a sprained ankle and a budding migraine, Jared the Jerk had moved in next door, and her summer job had flown the coop. She loved her position at the Tory Hills Elementary School, but it didn't pay well enough for her to afford a brand new car. Damn! If only Mary could have eloped before the interest rates on car loans had lowered so temptingly!

It wasn't just the money either, though Genna was almost a fanatic about financial security. She had been looking forward to her usual summer stint in the catering business. If she had one fantasy occupation, it was to be a chef. She loved to cook and bake and took great joy in creating wonderful meals and desserts. The summer was Mary's busy season because she specialized in catering outdoor affairs. Working with Mary had given Genna a chance to make a little extra cash and live out her fantasy.

Amy heaved a sigh that mixed relief with frustration. She had feared Genna would catch the suspicious tone in her voice and make her spill the beans, but Genna was staring glumly at a stack of bills. That was good, she thought, except that in a way she had wanted to spill the beans. Her mouth was just aching to blurt out that J. J. Hennessy had intercepted her in Genna's driveway and asked all sorts of questions about her.

She swiveled her head back in Genna's direction, her mop of blond curls bouncing, her smile sunny.

"Have you met our new neighbor?"

"Jared the Jerk, God's gift to women?"

Uh-oh. Amy kept her smile frozen firmly in place. "He's a nice guy, Gen. I know he comes on a little like—"

"A jackhammer," Genna supplied.

"I'll admit he's a little . . . different—"

"He's an oddity." She said it as if she were saying "he's a toad."

Amy bit her lip and tried to regroup her thoughts. "So he's a little . . . flamboyant," she said, gesturing airily with her chubby hands. "But he's really sweet once you know him, and he's been unbelievably patient with the neighborhood kids. They've been hounding him day and night." A man who was good with kids would appeal to Genna, Amy realized.

"If he's so famous," Genna said, ignoring the obvious man-who's-good-with-kids ploy, "what's he doing in Tory Hills?"

"*If? If* he's so famous?" Amy questioned, incensed. "Genna, where have you been? J. J. Hennessy is *the* most famous quarterback! He ranks right up there with McMahon, Kramer, Simms, Montana. He put the Hawks on top. They won the *Super Bowl* last January!"

Amy had nearly died and gone to Hartford-Hawks heaven when she'd heard who was moving in across the street from her. How could Genna live on the same planet and be so indifferent?

"You know I don't follow sports, Amy," Genna said, pouting, as she doodled sad faces on the envelope of her electric bill with a ball-point pen.

Amy cast her gaze and hands heavenward. "His face has been on every major magazine cover: *Sports Illustrated, People, Playgirl.*"

Genna just shrugged and brushed back a lock of wavy, chin-length chestnut hair.

"He does commercials on television."

No response.

"He's been on *Donahue*, for Pete's sake!" she said shrilly.

"Enough about this guy, Amy," Genna complained. "Aren't you going to ask me about my vacation?"

Amy gritted her teeth but let the subject of J. J. Hennessy drop for the moment. She took a deep breath, forced a smile, and asked, "How was your vacation, Genna?"

"Hell on earth."

Genna still couldn't believe it herself. Who would've thought a week on Cape Cod would turn out to be like living out a Stephen King novel? Not Genna. She'd been looking forward to it for months. All she'd had to do was get through her cousin's wedding. After that she was going to lie in the sun on the patio of the hideously expensive beach cottage she'd scrimped and saved to rent and enjoy the peace and quiet while reading a stack of romance novels. But no . . .

"First there was Lauren's big surprise," she began. "My sweet cousin canceled my reservation and arranged for me to stay with her in-laws. I lost a sixty-dollar deposit."

Amy grimaced. "So what were the in-laws like?"

"Rich. Their summer house was just a few bobbing boats down the beach from the Kennedy place."

Amy's brown eyes almost popped out of her head as she went through the stack of photos Genna had shoved at her. She was looking at an estate complete with tennis courts and a private boat launch. "Holy buckets, this place looks like a Club Med! What the blue blazes are you whining about?"

"You'll see," Genna replied placidly. When Amy came to the wedding pictures, Genna pointed out the groom. "That's Robert. He's an investment banker from a long line of investment bankers. The Holmes-Cummingses were the investment bankers on the *Mayflower*."

"Was he born wearing pinstripes?"

"Yes. And when he smiles you can see that being born with a silver spoon in his mouth gave him the overbite of a parrot. But Lauren loves him and he's good to her. . . ."

Genna felt an undeniable twinge of envy. At thirty, she was the eldest of three daughters and the only one as yet unmarried. She wasn't holding out for an investment banker, or even a surgeon. She just wanted a nice, safe, normal kind of guy with a steady, normal job.

"You looked nice in your dress," Amy commented.

"Thanks." Genna frowned. "I've been maid of honor so many times, they're going to start calling me *old* maid of honor. If I had a dollar for every time my mother said, 'That's my Genna, always the bridesmaid, never the bride,' I could pay off the national debt. Then there was her oft-repeated explanation of her eldest daughter's unmarried state, complete with apologetic face and tragic blue eyes—'Genna is *career oriented.*' As if that were some sort of a birth defect!"

Abigail Hastings never said "Genna graduated summa cum laude," or "Genna is an excellent teacher." If Genna had become president of the United States, it wouldn't have impressed her mother half as much as her marrying a gynecologist and becoming secretary of the PTA.

That idea didn't sound so bad to Genna either, but she was proud of her accomplishments. She'd done a lot on her own. To her, a woman's worth was not contingent on her having a husband. That was icing on the cake. A person could have cake without icing; it just wasn't as sweet.

"Oh, yuck! Who is this?" Amy's disgusted voice brought Genna back to the present.

She smiled unpleasantly at the photo of a buck-toothed super nerd with Coke-bottle-lens glasses. "That, as Paul Harvey says, is the rest of the story. That is Cousin Lauren's cousin Rodney, who also answered to 'Dinner is served.' Rodney the instant migraine, the family oddball, my constant and unwelcomed companion for the entire week. He's a Roto-Rooter man."

Amy looked as if she'd just swallowed a bug.

"That about says it all." Genna nodded. "Did I mention he's on parole? He tried to rob Dunkin' Donuts with a gun carved from a bar of soap."

She proceeded to tell the tales of her misadventures with Rodney, which included swamping a sailboat, nearly falling overboard while on the Nantucket ferry, and spraining her ankle when Rodney mowed her down during a game of mixed doubles.

"So, that's the way of my life. My cousin marries a Holmes-Cummings and I am relentlessly pursued by a Roto-Rooter man."

"Poor Gen." Amy patted her friend's hand. "You need a vacation."

"Howdy, neighbor!" came J. J. Hennessy's voice through the screen door.

"Or a gun," Genna amended Amy's statement, her teeth gritting automatically at the thought of J.J.

Jared let himself in. He had changed into a pair of cutoffs and a blue Hawaiian print shirt that hung open over an orange T-shirt. He had a Red Sox cap turned backward on his head and was brandishing a measuring cup in one hand.

"Just come on in, Mr. Hennessy," Genna drawled sarcastically.

Amy grimaced at her tone but then caught the twinkle of amusement in Jared's eye. He was up to something.

"Nice pad you got here, Gen," he said, nodding approvingly as he looked around.

"I'm *so* glad you like it."

"Hey," he said as he grinned and shrugged, "it's you, gorgeous!"

The house had looked like a cracker box from the outside, but inside, the first floor was almost totally open, giving the illusion of space. The living room, dining room, and kitchen all flowed together, decorated in various shades of blue. The look was cozy and welcoming. It was the kind of place that would offer comfort and haven after a long day. It suited her, Jared thought, even if she didn't seem too welcoming herself at the moment.

Jared suppressed a chuckle. He was definitely getting her attention. Never mind that she looked ready to spit tacks. He had her emotions running high. Eventually he would turn that to his advantage.

Genna was a challenge. Not that Jared was conceited, but he usually had to beat women away with a stick. Now here was one that not only snarled at him, but practically sizzled when he touched her. She was a challenge all right, and Jared had been schooled from an early age to approach every challenge like the football field general he was. Strategy was the name of the game.

"Aren't you going to give Jared the grand tour?" Amy asked innocently. "I'm sure he'd enjoy seeing the loft."

Genna gave her smiling friend a meaningful scowl. She turned her attention then to her unwelcomed guest and asked, annoyed, "Did you come here to borrow something? The traditional cup of sugar, perhaps?"

"Naw." He leaned negligently across the counter that divided the kitchen and dining room, a teasing smile twitching the corners of his lips. "Too cliché for me. Do you have any coffee?"

"You want to *borrow* a cup of coffee? And you drink your coffee out of a measuring cup?"

He shrugged, an elegant lifting of his magnificent shoulders. His gorgeous eyes crinkled at the corners. "Why not? Live it up, Gen. Life's too boring. I'd prefer something with an international flavor if you have it—café au lait, mocha mint—"

Genna gritted her teeth and lied right through them. "I don't have any coffee."

"No coffee." He pretended to frown. "Frosted Flakes?"

Amy giggled, earning her a baleful glare from Genna.

"No."

"M&M's?" He tried a boyish grin. "They're my favorite."

"No, Mr. Hennessy."

He could almost hear the threads of her temper beginning to snap. He came around the counter and put a brotherly hand on her shoulder. Genna's hair nearly stood on end from the electricity that zinged between them.

"You don't have to call me mister, Gen. We're neighbors! J.J. or Jared, whichever you prefer."

Genna glared at him. "I prefer not to call you at all."

He mussed her hair and smiled. "You can call me a cab, but I won't pay the fare."

Peals of laughter that sounded like a flock of geese in a frenzy erupted from Amy.

Jared spotted the photo of Rodney on the table. "Hey, who's the Roto-Rooter man?"

Genna bit her lip.

Amy fell off her chair.

Two

"Of all the insufferable clods to have move in next door," Genna grumbled to herself as she settled on her lounge chair. She fluffed the pillow under her sore ankle, arranged the ice pack just so, then carefully eased her foot onto the pile. Leaning back on the smoke-blue flowered cushion, she adjusted her bikini top and picked up her book.

"I can't believe the nerve of that guy. Just walking into my house as big as life," she muttered after reading three sentences. *As big as life.* That phrase conjured up a memory of mile-wide shoulders and rippling muscles. She frowned. "So he's decent looking. So what?"

. . . sparkling ice-blue eyes, a wry, quirking mouth . . .

"Okay. Gorgeous. Big deal."

Three more sentences passed before her eyes.

"Arrogant doesn't even begin to describe him."

. . . humor in his eyes. Humor at what? Her? Himself? The folly of life?

She let the book in her hand dangle down near the red brick of her tiny patio. She couldn't remember the last time a man had flustered her as badly as J. J. Hennessy had. Rodney didn't count; he could almost be considered a lesser life form. Jared Hennessy was a man. All man. Every sexy inch of him.

A scowl pulled at Genna's features. Not only was he arrogant, she told herself, he was obviously an irresponsible goof-off. Not her type at all. Anybody could tell that just by looking at him. Where did he shop for his clothes, rummage sales? He probably thought Brooks Brothers was a comedy act.

A football player. Huh. That said it all, didn't it? He must be about thirty going on seventeen. A man playing a boy's game for a living. The word responsibility was undoubtedly absent from his vocabulary.

With him living next door she was definitely going to have to invest in high blood pressure medication. It had been hours since the scene in her kitchen, and she could still hear her pulse pounding in her ears when she thought of him. He had to be the most obnoxious man in the tri-state area.

Then why do your hormones go into overdrive when he touches you, Genna?

"Oh, shut up," she muttered to the annoying little voice in her head.

Suddenly something cold and wet was nudging her hand. Genna's eyes went huge with fright and she jerked her head around. Two china blue eyes stared up at her from the face of a fat, furry black and white puppy. He sat perfectly still, waiting for her reaction. Genna laughed her relief, which the puppy took as a good sign. His tail wagged, wriggling his entire chubby body.

"You gave me a scare, little guy." She ruffled his thick fur. "You new in town?"

A hesitant movement halfway behind her chair caught Genna's eye as she leaned over to pet the puppy. She leaned over a little more, her brows lifting in surprise. At the edge of the patio stood a pretty little girl of about four or five, her tumble of thick black hair caught up in a ponytail with a crooked pink bow, her blue eyes filled with uncertainty.

Genna swung her legs over the side of the lounge and sat up. "Hi," she said, smiling. "I'll bet this puppy belongs to you."

The little girl nodded. She came no closer, though she cast a nervous glance at her errant pet. She looked ready to turn and run at a second's notice.

"He's a very nice puppy. What's his name?"

She seemed to be weighing the pros and cons of answering, as one hand tugged at the bottom of her pink and lavender top. She scuffed the toe of her pink and white sneaker on the patio brick. Finally she said, "Flurry."

Genna turned her attention to the dog. "Nice to meet you, Flurry. I'm Genna." She reached down and shook the puppy's paw. "Can you tell me your mistress's name?"

Silence. The puppy licked her hand enthusiastically.

"He can't talk," came the little voice. "Except dog talk."

"Really? I don't know much about puppies."

The little girl chewed her bottom lip, looked from Genna to Flurry and then over her shoulder. She took a small step forward. "My name's Alyssa."

"What a lovely name," Genna said. "Alyssa what?"

"Alyssa Hennessy."

Genna was certain the lounge had collapsed beneath her. Hennessy! With difficulty she found her voice and pointed to the gray house. "You live over there with your daddy and *mommy?*"

"With only my daddy," Alyssa said, her expression suddenly guarded.

A strange sort of relief flowed through Genna at the news that there was no Mrs. Hennessy in the house next door. Only because she hated to think of this darling little girl having a married father who played around on the side, she told herself. She still thought J.J. was short for Jumbo Jerk, but at least he wasn't *that* kind.

Without warning, the object of her thoughts rounded the corner of her garage. He was wearing the same strange outfit he'd had on earlier, but the expression on his face was completely different. He looked serious, worried even, then relieved as his gaze landed on his daughter.

"Alyssa—"

"I didn't wander, Daddy," she explained. "Flurry got away and I had to come and get him."

Jared kneeled down by his daughter and brushed back her black bangs. "Okay, muffin, but you should have come to get me first. What if Flurry had run to another block? You might have gotten lost."

Sudden tears swam in her huge blue eyes. "But he's *my* puppy."

Jared kissed her cheek. "That's right, sweetheart, and as soon as Uncle Cory gets here, we'll start building him a pen in our yard so he can't wander off."

Genna sat watching, astounded. Who was this guy? He certainly didn't resemble the overbearing Romeo she'd met. He looked up at her, catching her staring. She turned away, hoping he would think her blush was from the sun. She grabbed her yellow T-shirt and pulled it on to cover her bikini top. She guessed this action would earn her a smart remark from him. But he surprised her again.

"Sorry if we interrupted your sunning," Jared said, standing. He was even sorrier she'd covered herself. Under that oversized T were two lovely, full, round breasts. She was obviously modest though, as she wore cutoffs instead of the brief bottoms that went with the bikini top. Jared smiled inwardly. He even found her modesty appealing. Not as appealing as her body, but certainly refreshing.

"No—a—" Genna stammered. Even his voice was different now, softer, more velvety. She dropped her gaze to the little girl and puppy. "Alyssa and Flurry and I were just getting acquainted."

"Genna's nice, Daddy," Alyssa said with a shy smile, tucking her hand into her father's much larger one.

Jared glanced at his daughter, then turned twinkling eyes on Genna. "I know."

Genna was suddenly awash with goose bumps. Out of nervousness she rose, careful not to put too much weight on her sore ankle. "I was just about to bring out some fresh-baked chocolate chip cookies. Would you two care to join me?"

"Can we, Daddy?"

Jared looked long and hard at Genna. He'd thrown her a curve, and she wasn't sure how to handle it.

Good. He smiled. Keep her off balance. "Sure. I'll help you."

In the kitchen Genna fussed unnecessarily with plates and napkins, arranging the cookies on a tray. What should she say to him? She knew how to handle a smart aleck, but this was a whole different ball game. Should she apologize for her behavior earlier, or what? And she was dying to know the circumstances of Jared's single parenthood, but she couldn't bring herself to just come right out and ask him. He saved her the trouble.

"Lyssa's mom and I split when she was one," he said, pouring milk into yellow plastic tumblers. "Elaine was killed in a car accident about six weeks ago."

"I'm sorry," she said, feeling even more at a loss. Had he been close to his ex-wife? Divorce didn't necessarily destroy a relationship entirely.

With Jared in this quiet mood, Genna felt a surprisingly strong desire to reach out to him and offer comfort, but uncertainty held her back.

"Yeah," he went on, looking out the window above the sink, watching his daughter play with her puppy. "Lyssa was with her when it happened. She barely got a scratch, thank God."

Genna recalled the sudden closed look on Alyssa's face when she'd answered that she lived with her father. Poor little lamb. "That must have been terrible for her."

"Yeah," he said so softly she almost missed it.

"So Alyssa came to live with you."

"Yep." He turned back to her with a big false grin that didn't hide the vulnerability in his eyes. "That's me, Bachelor Father."

He took the tray bearing their snack and carried it out, leaving Genna to stare after him. Bachelor Father. That must cramp his style with the ladies, she mused. She looked out the window and saw him swing his little girl up in his arms, cuddle and kiss her, and Genna got the distinct impression Jared didn't mind at all.

They sat at Genna's round picnic table after Jared got

Alyssa washed up. Genna watched expectantly as he bit into a cookie. His eyes lit up and widened as he chewed.

"This is incredible!" he mumbled, still chewing.

Genna felt a rush of pride. Kitchen vanity. She loved to hear praise for her culinary skills. She knew darn well her chocolate chip specials were moist, rich, and chewy, with just the right consistency for dunking, but she could never hear enough of people telling her so.

"You actually made this? Jared questioned with reverent awe. "With your own two hands?"

"My own secret recipe." Genna beamed.

"Outstanding!" He grinned. He looked to his daughter for confirmation. "Great, huh, Lyss?"

An exuberant nod came from the little girl, who had chocolate all over her face.

"Do you do this for a living?" He knew from quizzing Amy that Genna was a teacher. He also knew about her scuttled summer job. But asking questions seemed like a good way to make conversation and get some ideas on how to win her over.

"No," Genna replied. "I teach kindergarten. Will you be in kindergarten this year, Alyssa?" She smiled beguilingly at the little girl.

Jared felt a twinge of envy. His daughter had effortlessly captured Genna's heart. Of course, Alyssa *was* an adorable little doll, he added silently with a father's pride.

Alyssa shrugged in answer. There had been so many upheavals in her life recently, Jared thought, the poor baby didn't know what to be sure of anymore. He nodded when Genna turned questioning eyes on him.

"Genna will be your teacher, Lyss. Won't that be neat?"

That shy, heart-stealing smile eased up the corners of Alyssa's mouth as she looked at Genna. "I know my numbers and the alphabet too."

"That's wonderful," Genna replied. "You'll be at the head of the class."

Alyssa nodded. "Uh-huh. I can print my name too. Daddy showed me."

Jared blushed a little at Genna's look of pleasant surprise. She felt a smile threaten as she pictured this football Adonis crouched over tiny Alyssa, patiently teaching her the abc's.

"You could make a fortune on these," he said, biting into another cookie.

Genna laughed, a sound he'd been waiting to hear. He wasn't disappointed. Her laughter was free and spontaneous, no practiced little twitter. "I've been making them for fifteen years, and so far all I've gained is weight."

He chuckled and leered comically. "In all the right places, I'd say."

It was Genna's turn to blush. She hurried to change the subject. "Actually, I usually do some cooking professionally during the summer, but my friend packed up her catering business and moved, so . . ."

"So you're out of a job?" He had been racking his brain to come up with a job to offer her, but hadn't had much luck. He was sure she'd turn down the housekeeper ploy, and just baby-sitting for Alyssa wouldn't pay well enough.

"I'll have to start looking for something Monday." She wondered if Betsy Franke could use an extra cook now that she had inherited Mary's summer bookings.

"Well, if you ever decide to go into the bakery business let me know," Jared said. "I'm always looking for a good investment. These cookies are a sure thing."

"Flurry likes them too, Genna," Alyssa announced as the puppy snatched the offered treat and wagged his tail as he gulped it down.

A red Porsche pulled up in front of Jared's house and the horn sounded, playing Charge!

"Uncle Cory!" Alyssa squealed, climbing off the bench. She dashed away with Flurry hot on her heels.

"That's my weekend construction crew," J.J. said, standing. He sent Genna one of his patented grins. "Thanks for the cookies, Teach. Catch you later."

With that he was gone. Genna chewed thoughtfully on a cookie. It seemed she had more than one neighbor: a macho madman, and a bachelor father with a velvet voice and vulnerable blue eyes.

"Will the real Jared Hennessy please stand up?"

A doghouse that was a miniature White Castle hamburger stand? Genna shook her head in disbelief as she sat at a white wrought iron table on Jared's patio staring at the ridiculous structure. Unbelievable. The whole scene was unbelievable.

The summer sun beat down on the crowd in the backyard. Rock music blared from a boom box hanging from the limb of a white oak tree. More people were dancing than working, though two men were planting fence posts around the perimeter of the yard *and* dancing. The chain-link fence they were putting up was going to be ordinary enough, not so the miniature pink flamingos stuck in the ground around the doghouse. Further testimony to the abnormality of the man, Genna told herself.

She looked at Jared, who was dancing with two little neighborhood girls, his daughter on his broad shoulders. Half the town of Tory Hills was partying here. There were enough beer and soda cans in the trash to build a DeLorean.

Was it going to be this way every weekend? she wondered, frowning. She had never been much of a party girl and she didn't want to start now. She loved quiet weekends at home. Was J. J. Hennessy to be the end of them?

She took a sip of the beer Jared had plunked down in front of her and gagged. How had she allowed Amy to drag her here? She couldn't remember, but she certainly remembered her way home, and that's where she was heading. She stood and reached for her crutches, only to have them deftly swept away by Jared. He leaned a denim-clad hip on the table.

"Leaving so soon, Teach?" he asked with a grin. "Where's your party mania?"

"I don't have any," she answered flatly.

"Ah." He frowned in mock seriousness. "A party mania deficiency. An adjustment to your biological party barometer is in order. Let's see what we've got here."

Genna watched him search through the many pockets and loops of his cutoff bib overalls and pull out five screwdrivers, three pliers, a hammer, a toothbrush, a lint brush, a can opener, a bottle opener, and seven ball-point pens.

"Have enough tools in there?" she asked wryly as he inspected one contraption after another.

Jared leered at her. "All the important ones."

Genna grimaced at the lewd remark, trying not to notice the ripple of bare chest and arm muscles as he extracted what looked like a tire pressure gauge and came toward her with it.

"Now, just let Dr. J.J. take care of you—"

"You touch me with that thing and you won't have a tool left in working order," she snarled, face-to-face with his hard chest.

"J.J., where are the extra potato chips?" a buxom blonde with legs up to her armpits asked on her way to the house. She wore red silk shorts and a Hawks T-shirt that gave new meaning to the word "skintight." She was one of the Lady Hawks, the team cheerleaders.

"In the cupboard, the third door to the left of the microwave."

"Think she can count that far?" Genna asked sweetly.

Jared's eyes glittered with dangerous amusement. "I hope so. She's an associate professor at the University of Connecticut."

Genna felt about three inches tall. Her mouth dropped open. She closed it, then ventured meekly, "Phys ed?"

"Differential calculus. Can't judge a book by its cover, Teach. Isn't that part of the kindergarten curriculum anymore?"

Genna scowled and looked out at the party. She'd been bitchy and small-minded, which wasn't at all like her. And worse yet, for some reason she cared very much that Jared Hennessy not think badly of her.

"I learned that in kindergarten," he went on, swilling her beer. "That and how to play doctor."

She slanted him a disgusted look. "Anything else?"

He looked thoughtful a moment and nodded. "That l-m-n-o-p is not all one letter."

She came dangerously close to giggling at that. Damn the man! Just when she was sure she despised him, he did something to make her laugh.

"So what do you think of the doghouse?" he asked, casting a proud smile at the canine castle.

"I only hope no one mistakes it for a drive-in. Couldn't you have done something a little more . . . colonial?" she offered, trying not to hurt his feelings. "To go with the house."

"Mmmm," he said thoughtfully. "I tried scaling down Mount Vernon but the wings took up too much yard space. Besides, I don't want Flurry getting the wrong idea and thinking he can invite overnight guests, at least not until he's neutered."

"Hey, Hennessy!" The booming voice came from a teammate called Brutus, who was roughly the size of Mount McKinley. Brutus wore his hair in a Mohawk and his body encased in black leather. He looked like someone from a Mad Max movie. From halfway across the yard he flung a foaming can of beer at Jared, who snagged it inches from Genna's head—but not before it sprayed her face and soaked the front of her plaid blouse.

Laughing, Jared shook the can hard and fired it back at Brutus, who caught it and spiked it on the ground like a football, then went into a victory dance.

"Touchdown!" Jared yelled, dancing around the table, "All right, Brutus!"

Genna stood, sputtering, trying to wipe the beer off her face with her hands. She wondered if anyone had ever done any serious studies on the placement of athletes on the evolutionary scale.

Brutus picked up the can, poured the last of the beer down his throat from an arm's length away, then tore the can in two with his teeth.

"That guy is missing a chromosome," she said as Jared danced around her doing things with his hips that threatened to give her palpitations.

"Brutus? He's just having fun. Don't you know anything about having fun?"

"I know all about having fun," she said primly. "It has nothing to do with recycling aluminum orally."

"It does to Brutus. I don't know about you, but *I'm* not telling him any different."

At the edge of the patio a game of Nerf football had turned ugly. Two players were wrestling on the ground rubbing barbecue briquettes into each other's faces. The dog ran by with a flamingo clenched in his teeth. Two perfect examples of why I shouldn't be here, Genna thought to herself, her temper wearing thin. She tried to blow beer-damp bangs off her forehead as she plucked the wet fabric of her blouse off her chest.

The Nerf ball squirted up out of the pile of humanity on the lawn, bounced off Genna's forehead, and into Jared's hands. He tossed it out to Kyle Dennison, who was promptly tackled by a dozen neighborhood kids.

"Know anything about football, Gen?" J.J. asked, still dancing. He draped a muscular arm across her shoulders, his gyrating hips bumping hers.

"Certainly," she said stiffly, trying to ignore the tingles racing through her as he brushed against her. "It's a game played by enormous, sweating men who spit and scratch—"

"That's baseball," he corrected.

"And wear Joan Crawford shoulder pads," Genna continued, her fuse burning down to the short fibers. "It's violent and stupid, and I'd rather have a pelvic exam than be forced to watch it on TV."

She snatched her crutches up and started for home.

Piqued by Genna's unflattering description of his chosen profession, Jared stood stiffly and watched her hobble across the lawn. It wasn't going to further his cause any, but he couldn't resist the urge to take her down a peg or two. He waited until she was halfway home before yelling, "Yeah, well, I still want you in my Jacuzzi, gorgeous!"

For one horrible eternity every pair of eyes at the party riveted on Genna. It seemed even the flamingos were staring at her. She could feel their eyes burning into her back.

Death by slow torture would be too good for him, she thought, taking back all the feelings of contrition she'd had Friday afternoon. She was definitely sticking to her original opinion of him: J. J. Hennessy was an arrogant, mannerless, macho swine. A *gorgeous, sexy,* arrogant, mannerless, macho swine. And she was absolutely certain she wanted nothing to do with him. Almost.

He is not normal, she reminded herself as she limped around her kitchen slamming pots and pans onto the counter. She'd had her fill of crazy people when she was growing up. All of her father's family was certifiable, her father included. A self-proclaimed inventor, he'd chased one harebrained scheme after another until he dropped dead, leaving his family with nothing but debts and not even a cent of insurance. He'd been an overgrown boy with no concept of responsibility. Just like J. J. Hennessy.

"Why'd you leave the party, Gen?" Amy whined, letting herself in the kitchen door.

Genna opened the refrigerator and started flinging vegetables into the sink. Potatoes sailed through the air one at a time, arching gracefully into the porcelain basin. A bunch of carrots missed the target and skidded down the counter, sliding into a piece of salt-glazed stoneware. Scallions flew like scattering buckshot. Amy dodged a stalk of celery. Genna answered without coming out of the refrigerator. "I won't be a party to madness."

"Lighten up. A little madness is good for a person." Leaning around Genna, she snatched a Coke out of the fridge and plopped down on a stool at the counter.

"Who are you now, Dr. Joyce Brothers?" Genna shot her friend a glare as she returned to the sink and started peeling carrots with a vengeance.

"It didn't take a shrink to see you weren't trying very hard to have fun," Amy answered.

"You shouldn't have to try if it's fun," Genna said without turning around. "I don't happen to like mass insanity, and the taste of beer turns my mouth inside out."

Suddenly suspicious, Amy asked, "What are you making?"

"Vegetable soup."

"But it's ninety degrees out!"

"I'll freeze it."

"You're upset, Genna," she singsonged in her grating voice, a self-satisfied smirk on her face.

"I am not upset." Genna stabbed a potato with her paring knife.

"You always cook when you're upset."

Genna spun around with the knife clutched in her hand, her eyes wild. The beer in her bangs had dried, leaving them stiff and straight as string. The front of her blouse was one big stain. *"I am not upset!"*

Amy smiled serenely and drummed her fingers on the counter. "Not at all. Are those chocolate chip cookies over there?"

Glaring at the clear glass cookie jar, Genna said nothing. One jar of cookies was hardly proof. Thank heaven Amy didn't know about the three frozen cakes. She turned and calmly attacked a stalk of celery.

"Wasn't it nice of J.J. to invite everyone over? He's so sweet—"

"He's a lunatic." Chop. Chop. Chop.

"I'll bet he signed a hundred autographs this afternoon."

"He's a spectacle." Stab. Stab. Stab.

"He's got style."

Genna faced her friend with an exasperated look. "The man mows his lawn in stripes and puts pink flamingos around the doghouse."

"I said he had style," Amy qualified. "I never said anything about taste."

They were silent for a moment while Genna dumped her mutilated vegetables into a big stockpot and set it on the stove to simmer. Amy sipped her soda, waiting for Genna to turn toward her so she could watch her friend's expression when she dropped her bomb.

"I think he's interested in you, Gen. As in 'romance.' "

Something akin to panic flashed across Genna's face, then changed into annoyance. "I think he's interested in most of the unmarried female population of Connecticut."

"Are you attracted to him?"

"Certainly not," she said huffily. She turned back to her cupboards and started rummaging through them. How could she be attracted to a macho lunkhead like him? Absurd.

"Come on!" Amy scoffed. "The guy's got a bod to die for!"

"He's moderately good looking . . . in a brutish sort of way," Genna said grudgingly, her blood heating up at the thought of his muscular arm draped across her shoulders, his lean hip bumping hers. Those gorgeous, translucent blue eyes took her breath away, and he had a smile that could melt stone. Tom Selleck should be so good looking.

Amy snorted. "It seems to me you're trying pretty darn hard not to like him."

It was Genna's turn to snort as she ripped open packages of yeast and dumped them into a bowl of hot water. "I don't have to try not to like him. It comes naturally."

"Bull." Amy plucked a cookie from the jar and munched on it. "I think you know he's a hunk and a half."

"Ha!"

"I think you know it, and it turns you on, and that's why you're upset."

"I am not upset!" Genna shouted, flinging flour into the bowl, a cloud of white dust rising to coat her hair and face.

"What are you doing there?"

"Making bread."

"Oh, good day for it," Amy said dryly, reaching for a second cookie. "You can put it out on the driveway to bake."

Genna snarled as she took a wooden spoon to the batter.

"Careful, you'll dislocate your shoulder."

Sometimes Genna wished Amy weren't such a good friend. Amy never hesitated to say what was on her mind, and no amount of nasty looks or sarcastic remarks could drive her away if she didn't want to be driven.

Neither woman spoke for several minutes. The sounds of the party came in through the screen door. Someone was getting thrown into the kiddie pool.

"Genna, are you afraid to try another relationship because of what happened with Allan?" Amy asked gently. She winced as she saw her friend flinch at the name. Damn Allan Corrigan to hell and gone, Amy thought.

The pain was automatic, a conditioned response, but Genna had a firm hold on her emotions when she answered. "No. But that doesn't mean I'm desperate either. I don't have to throw myself at the first guy to come along."

"J.J.'s hardly the first guy to express an interest."

"He's an irresponsible playboy who wants only to get me in his Jacuzzi!" Her hands squeezed the bread dough. She pretended she was strangling Jared Hennessy. It had to be his fault she wanted him and wanted him gone all at the same time.

"I don't think that's true," Amy said, "but it sounds like fun just the same."

"He's not my type," Genna said stubbornly.

"You and your blasted type!" Amy said disgustedly, banging her Coke can on the counter. "You don't want a man. You want a three-piece suit and a subscription to *The Wall Street Journal*."

"I want someone who's quiet and loyal—"

"Springer spaniels are quiet and loyal," Amy commented sardonically. "I don't think they shed much either."

Genna turned around and glowered at her pudgy friend. "There's nothing wrong with looking for a person with certain qualities."

"No, there's nothing wrong with that," Amy agreed. "There's nothing wrong with having a little fun either.

You're a fun person, Gen. What are you going to do with Mr. Dull N. Boring when you find him?"

Unable to come up with any kind of suitable answer, Genna turned back to her dough and slugged it.

Amy slid off her stool and headed back toward the party, stopping at the kitchen door. "I don't think that's what you want at all, but you've convinced yourself that's the kind of man you need to feel safe. Do yourself a favor, Gen. Live it up. Have a summer fling."

Genna walked to the screen door as she wiped her hands on a blue striped towel. She watched Amy cross her lawn and rejoin the festivities next door. There was Jared, wearing a sombrero, dancing with a flamingo in each hand.

"So he's a hunk. Why should I care? Why should that upset me? It doesn't. He could be ten hunks and it wouldn't bother me," she said resolutely.

She chewed her bottom lip as she watched the sun gild a male body that should have been a bronze sculpture. Amy said she was looking for a man she would feel safe with. What was wrong with that? Nothing. She certainly wouldn't feel safe with Jared. A nun wouldn't feel safe with Jared.

"Maybe I should bake a cake as long as I've got the flour out."

Three

Jared stared down at the letter in his hands. A feeling he had experienced only rarely in his nine years in the NFL slashed through him like a knife. Fear. He hated it, resented it, but couldn't stop it from tearing his insides apart.

The letter, neatly typed on ivory vellum, was from Simone Harcourt, his ex-wife's older sister. He'd met her only a handful of times, but he'd spent enough time with her to have formed a lasting opinion: she was a cold, determined woman who despised him. The letter that trembled in his hands was absolute confirmation of that.

Simone didn't believe he was fit to be Alyssa's only parent. She didn't believe his lifestyle provided a suitable environment for a five-year-old girl. She claimed it was public knowledge that he was dedicated to decadence and that a life of parties and loose women did not hold a place for a child. She was prepared to take action—legal action—to see to it that Alyssa was spared the horrible fate of growing up under a playboy's influence.

A shudder jerking his body, Jared drove a hand through his close-cropped hair and swore. He swore until he couldn't think of any more curses, even though he was trying to give up the bad habit. He had vowed to quit swearing when Alyssa had come to live with him. The thought pulled a wry laugh from his throat.

He rubbed his hand over his face, then looked at the Super Bowl ring on his finger. It was large and impressive, the ultimate symbol of success in his profession. He was at the top, the pinnacle of his career. He was a celebrity, respected by his peers, and he had more money than he knew what to do with. He would gladly have given it all to the next stranger to come down the street if it meant keeping his baby girl with him.

When he'd married Elaine he hadn't been ready to settle down, but she had gotten pregnant and he had done the right and honorable thing. From the start their marriage had gone awry. Elaine had continually derided him for his freewheeling lifestyle—which she had enjoyed as much as he before their marriage. Rebellious, he had refused to give it up just as he had never given up the idea that Elaine had gotten pregnant because the idea of being married to a pro quarterback had appealed to her.

Less than two years after their marriage, Jared had given her a generous divorce settlement and walked out of her life, returning only to pick up his daughter for his regular visits specified in their separation agreement. He and Elaine had managed to destroy whatever fragile feelings they had had for each other, but one infinitely precious gift of their relationship remained. Alyssa. Leaving her was the only thing he regretted about his divorce; she was the only good thing he had to say about his marriage.

Jared heaved a sigh, carrying the letter and a Bullwinkle tumbler half full of Irish whiskey out onto the front porch. He sat on the step and stared out at his striped lawn, feeling helpless.

Sometimes he believed he'd stayed in the fast lane all these years just to spite Elaine. Or maybe it just had taken him this long to grow up. Whatever the reason, he'd become disenchanted this past year. He was tired of city life, night life, and being the life of the party. He'd changed his priorities, matured. He was ready to settle down. He wanted a real home, a dog, a wife maybe. And his daughter. More than anything, he wanted his daughter.

Would Simone Harcourt really be able to take her away from him?

What could he do to prevent it?

Twilight was gathering around Tory Hills. Jared swatted a mosquito on his arm and breathed deep the scent of newly mowed grass coming from the Ralstons' lawn next door. In his own yard two squirrels chased each other up and down the birch trees. Across the street, Michael Dennison, Amy and Brian's oldest son, was going after their shrubbery with a hedge trimmer. A silver car turned the corner at the end of the block. Genna.

J.J.'s secret agent—Amy—had told him Genna was heading into Hartford today in search of a summer job. After nearly a week of searching, she'd struck out in Tory Hills and the nearby Hartford suburbs.

He knew how she felt. He wasn't doing so hot trying to win her over. Half the time she looked at him as though he were a piece of meat gone bad. Then he would manage to crack through her defensive line and make her laugh, only to have her pull away from him. He was reasonably certain she was attracted to him physically, but that didn't cut much ice with a lady like Genna, especially since she seemed determined to keep her distance from him.

Amy had hinted that Genna's reluctance was the result of a soured relationship. If that was the case, he'd have to tread carefully. He needed to win her trust. If only he could think of a way to help her out that would keep her around so he could figure out how to gain some yards toward winning her heart.

The evening breeze fluttered the letter in his hand.

Suddenly inspiration hit him over the head like a baseball bat. If his plan worked, he would end up with custody of his daughter and Genna too. *You're a genius, Hennessy.*

Genna's car came up the driveway and disappeared into her garage. Minutes later Genna came out looking like a wilted flower, her pink linen suit limp and wrinkled, a dejected frown on her face. Even her usually bouncy chestnut hair looked sad and droopy. Jared's heart went out to her. He wanted to take her in his arms and kiss her and cheer her up.

"Hey, Genna!" he yelled, standing up. He didn't want to leave the porch for fear Alyssa would wake up and he wouldn't be able to hear her. "Come on over!"

Genna groaned. Why him? Why tonight? "Why me?" she muttered, limping across Jared's lawn with her pink pumps dangling from one hand.

"Where are your crutches?" he asked, concerned.

"They didn't go with my outfit," she said wearily, leaning against a white pillar. She felt like a dishrag and was sure she looked like one too. She really wasn't up to J.J. tonight.

Shooting her a look of reproach, he dropped to his knees on the sidewalk, his hands tenderly examining her nylon-clad ankle. "It's puffy. Hot too. You really shouldn't be walking on it, especially in heels."

"Yeah, well, I might as well get used to it, because walking is going to be the way I'll get around if I don't find a job."

Jared stood and leaned against the same pillar with his hands stuffed into his pockets. "No luck, huh?"

"The word doesn't belong in my vocabulary."

He bit his lip. She sounded so depressed. Poor thing. He almost felt guilty at being glad she hadn't found a job. Almost.

"I know what you need," he said, his eyes twinkling.

Genna eyed him suspiciously. He was wearing baggy khaki shorts and a pink T-shirt that said REAL MEN EAT QUICHE AT FRANCESCA'S. "Don't pull out a tool on me, Jared. I'm liable to kill you with it."

He laughed, his diamond earring sparkling in the twilight. "Now don't get homicidal on me, Gen." He picked Candy the mannequin off her lawn chair and dumped her unceremoniously on a shrub. "Pull up a chair. I'll be right back."

He dashed into the house and returned thirty seconds later with two cold soft drink cans.

"Root beer?" Genna questioned, accepting the can and sinking down gratefully onto the lawn chair.

"Nothing beats the blues better." He sat on the porch floor facing her, leaning back against a pillar with one long leg dangling down the step, the other knee drawn up. "It's my secret passion. You have any secret passions, Gen?"

"Hmmm?" She found her gaze drawn to an alluring gap in the leg of his shorts. Was he the underwear type or not? Abruptly she realized he was waiting for an answer. She blushed furiously. "No. None."

He grinned and swigged his root beer. "I have to confess, I'm sort of glad you didn't find a job today, because I have a proposition for you."

Genna sat stock-still, afraid to let her imagination loose to decipher his comment.

Jared's smile died a slow death as he picked up Simone Harcourt's letter and tapped it on his knee, trying to think of the best way to phrase his offer. "I—a—I'm in kind of a bind. I need an image consultant."

"An image consultant? I don't understand." She was too innately polite to agree with him right off the bat. Besides, he seemed perfectly happy with the image he had, bizarre as it was.

"This letter is from my ex-wife's sister. She wants custody of Alyssa," he said, all humor gone from his voice.

"What?" Genna felt as if she'd suddenly had the wind knocked out of her. Despite what she claimed to think of Jared, she knew he adored his daughter. She'd watched him play with Alyssa in their backyard the last few days. He was endlessly patient with her, gentle and tender. Maybe he was a little too indulgent, but that was to be expected under the circumstances. He never looked at that little girl with anything but love in his eyes. It was there now as he looked up at Genna, love for his daughter, and that hint of vulnerability that tugged at Genna's heart so.

"She doesn't think I'm a fit parent."

"Not a fit parent?" she asked with indignation.

"She doesn't think I'm 'normal' enough."

"Uh-oh," Genna thought out loud.

He gave a harsh laugh. "You don't think so either?"

"It's not that I agree with her," she hastened to clarify. "I think you do a fine job with Alyssa. It's just that you're not . . . normal. I'm sorry."

"That's okay," he said, sighing. "You're right."

He sat up, leaned his elbows on his knees, and rubbed the back of his neck. "I know I'm not normal. I've never had to be. Nobody in my family is what you would call average. But I don't see why that should matter. I really want to settle down, you know. That's why I brought Alyssa here. I thought a small town, a big house, a lawn—that's how I want my daughter to grow up." He reached out and absently stroked the head of a flamingo. "I believe in individuality, but I need to fit in, Genna. I have to learn how to be normal, at least appear normal, or I could lose my little girl."

The strain in his voice on those last words almost broke Genna's heart.

J.J. turned toward her with hope in his eyes. "You're a teacher. You're normal. You need a job . . ."

She caught on to the direction of his thoughts and shook her head. "Oh, no. Not me."

How could she take on a job like that, be with him every day without succumbing to this weird attraction she had to him? Yes, she had finally decided to be honest enough with herself to admit she was attracted, but she still couldn't stand him.

"Please, Gen."

"No. Really, Jared, shouldn't you hire a man for the job?"

"No!" He abandoned his root beer and got on his knees in front of her lawn chair. One big hand wrapped around her wrist as he gestured with the other. "You're perfect for the job! Women are always telling men what to do!"

"Not this woman." Not that she wasn't tempted. She thought of Eve—she'd been tempted and look what had happened to her. Of course, a little voice nagged her, succumbing to this temptation probably wasn't going to sentence all of humanity to eternal damnation or anything. She steeled herself, shutting out the little voice. "No."

"Come on, Gen," Jared begged unashamedly, his thumb stroking Genna's wrist. "It's the perfect job for you. You don't have to dress up or drive to work. You could set your own hours. It'd be for only the summer."

She was getting a crick in her neck from shaking her head.

"You'd be getting paid to boss me around." He could tell she was tempted, like a fish eyeing a lure. Patience, J.J., he reminded himself. He gave her a devilish smile. "Wouldn't that be fun?"

Genna tried without great success to take a steadying breath. She felt as if he had his hand around her throat instead of around her wrist.

"I have to admit it holds a certain appeal . . . but . . . no, I'm sorry." She tore her gaze away from his smile and congratulated herself on regaining her self-control. "I just don't think it would be a good idea."

Jared reined in his impatience. No one ever caught a fish by yanking the bait away. His grandfather had told him that. His grandfather had also pointed out the similarities between fishing for trout and attracting a woman. He offered up silent thanks now to Grampa Jace for his lessons.

Jared eyed Genna shrewdly, looking for the weakness in her defense system. Under his thumb her pulse was racing like a rabbit's. "What are you afraid of, Gen?" he asked, knowing he'd hit the mark when she practically bolted. "It's a good honest job offer," he said to reassure her. *Slow and easy, J.J., don't scare her off.* "It's not like I'm asking you to marry me or anything."

"Afraid?" she laughed hysterically. "Why would I be afraid?"

Scared witless, maybe. But wasn't she adult enough to control her own responses around him? Of course she was. And he'd said himself that he wasn't asking her to marry him. He probably wasn't interested in her as a woman at all. Men like Jared never were. She was too ordinary and sensible.

Even if he were interested, she told herself, she would just explain to him that he wasn't her type. Simple. No problem.

She thought of the stack of bills on her dining room table. This was a genuine job offer. Lord knew it was the only one she'd had. What would be worse—spending every day with Jared or having her car repossessed?

"Fifteen hundred dollars salary," he offered.

"Fifteen hundred?"

"Two thousand."

"Two thousand!"

"Twenty-five hundred. I'll pay the taxes on it at the end of the year too. And an unlimited budget to make me into Normal Norman."

Genna's head swam. Twenty-five hundred dollars. That would cover a lot of car payments. And wouldn't it be fun to make Jared mow his lawn properly and get rid of the flamingos and the punk hair?

"You're perfect for the job, being a teacher and living right next door. You know the neighborhood. You know what the PTA types think of as good, normal parent material. And we're friends—sort of—aren't we?"

"I guess." Damn, he made a good argument. Those eyes of his should be declared lethal weapons, she thought, as the expression in his beautiful baby blues became soft and pleading.

"I need your help to keep my little girl," he said huskily. He was dead serious about the job. If Genna could coach him through a successful summer season of being normal enough to please the custody court, he'd give her every cent he had. Spending time with her was just going to be a bonus for him. "Please, Genna."

His free hand landed on her knee. Lightning went straight to her heart, then exploded and zipped down her arms and legs. The sensation excited her breasts and swirled between her thighs. Her heart raced, her breath caught in her throat. Their gazes locked. So much for controlling her own responses.

"No," she gasped, a feeble attempt at self-preservation.

A plaintive cry from inside the house broke the negotiations. Jared was on his feet and through the door before the second call of "Daddy." Concerned, Genna followed him to Alyssa's room.

Jared flipped a switch that lit a carousel lamp beside the white canopied bed. "What is it, sweetheart?" he asked, sitting on the edge of the bed and taking his sleep-dazed daughter in his arms.

"I don't feel good," Alyssa whined, pressing her head against his shoulder.

J.J. frantically felt her forehead for a sign of fever. "Where don't you feel good, honey?"

"My tummy."

He looked up at Genna, his face a mask of concern. "It's her tummy. Do you think it's her appendix? It could be her appendix."

A veteran in dealing with the maladies of five-year-olds, Genna came forward calmly and bent over them, brushing Alyssa's bangs back. "What'd you have for supper, honey?"

"Sausage-anchovy pizza and a chocolate shake," Jared answered.

Genna stared at him in horror.

He looked wild. "It had something from all the food groups!"

She shook her head and sighed resignedly. "I'll take the job."

After they had Alyssa settled back in bed with her doll and a tummy full of antacid, Jared walked Genna out onto the porch. Night had draped its black cloak across the sky and sprinkled it with stars. The corner streetlamp's pale silver light didn't quite make it to Jared's house. He settled his hands on Genna's shoulders and smiled down at her with his warm, winning smile.

"Thanks. You're a life saver."

"I think most people would have thought of antacid," Genna said, trying unsuccessfully to ignore the magnetic pull of his body.

Jared's mouth twitched at the corners. "I don't mean

just that. I mean about helping me become normal. I can't begin to tell you how grateful I am."

He moved closer, one hand wandering under her hair to caress the nape of her neck. Genna shivered. She thought she should make an appropriate employer-employee type statement, but the inside of her mouth had turned to sand, and she couldn't do anything but gaze mutely up at him.

He inched closer still, until his thighs were nearly brushing hers. He lowered his head at an angle as his glittering ice-blue eyes held hers captive. When he spoke, his voice had the same texture as the night sky. "I can't tell you, but maybe I can show you."

Genna told herself she should voice a protest as she tipped her head back and parted her lips, but that was impossible and she knew it. For some insane reason she wanted Jared Hennessy to kiss her. She wanted to know what it was like to be held by those muscular arms.

Jared was more than happy to show her. He gathered her against him, and his lips stole across hers in a teasing caress that had her arching up to him, silently begging for more. His hand cupped the back of her head, the silk of her hair threading through his fingers. His mouth slanted across hers, tasting, savoring her sweetness.

Genna moaned deep in her throat. His kiss was overwhelming. Not demanding, but a wonderful experience that sent her senses racing. She felt tiny and soft and feminine against Jared's rock-solid body. The heat his mouth generated against hers poured over her until she felt like a caramel that had been left out in the sun to melt.

Her hands set off on a journey that began at his lean, hard waist and wandered up the steep outward slope of his rib cage, then around and over the ridges and planes of muscle on his broad back. His body was a work of art. She felt as if she were caressing Michelangelo's *David*.

Reluctantly Jared lifted his head and let an inch or two of cool night air separate their bodies. Genna wasn't indifferent to him at all, he rejoiced inwardly. He had wanted the kiss to go on forever, but he'd felt his body responding to the sensual stimulus and had had enough sense to back off. Genna might not have fought off his kiss, but she was trying to fight the attraction that sparked between them. He wasn't going to push her. He had his fish on the hook now and he knew better than to lose her by reeling her in too fast. They'd be working together. She'd get to know him—and like him, he hoped. Gazing down into the surprise and confusion in her eyes, he realized how important that was to him.

"See you tomorrow, Teach." He smiled and backed toward the screen door.

Genna's tingling mouth formed the words "good night," but no sound issued forth. She offered him a weak smile and a nod.

" 'Night, Genna," he said huskily, slipping into his house.

Genna wasn't so sure she had enough control of her motor skills to get across their respective lawns. She wasn't altogether certain she wasn't going to keel over right there and then. Picking up her pink pumps, she limped toward her house feeling as if she'd just jumped into the rapids above Niagara Falls.

Turn Jared Hennessy into a normal person? Jared, with the diamond earring and striped lawn and kisses that sapped the strength from the knees of a perfectly controlled woman?

What on earth had she gotten herself into?

Four

"First of all, what do you know about being normal?" Genna asked, her pencil poised. She sat at Jared's kitchen table with a yellow legal pad in front of her, the top page covered with notes.

Jared stared into space with a look of intense concentration. He bit his lip and shifted on his chair like a teenager who'd gone to the ball game instead of reading his social studies assignment. Finally his gaze returned to Genna. "Nothing."

"Nothing at all?" she questioned, a tad dismayed. It would take more than giving Jared a haircut and getting the mannequin off his porch to impress a judge. She had hoped he would at least have a passing knowledge of basic normal behavior.

Maybe he did and just didn't realize it. She decided to throw out some questions that the average small-town person would know. "Just jump in when you have an answer. What's the best day to hit a garage sale? When do you fertilize the lawn? What do you wear to a PTA meeting? What's the best way to get rid of door-to-door salesmen? How many Brownies make a troop?"

He shook his head and shrugged.

Genna sighed. She didn't know anything about custody cases—they would know more when Jared's lawyer called back—but if it was anything like adoption, the court would send someone to report on Jared. They definitely had their work cut out for them if he was going to pass inspection.

"Well," she said, "the first order of business is to get you a housekeeper. Someone to cook and clean and keep an eye on Alyssa when you leave the house."

"I'd never leave Alyssa alone." He plucked another blueberry muffin out of the basket Genna had come armed with. Steam rose from it as he broke it open and spread butter on it. "Just what would having a house-keeper entail? Does she have to live here?"

"No."

"I don't want some fussy old bag taking over with Alyssa." He didn't always get her braids straight and he wasn't really up on the latest fashions for five-year-olds, but those were duties he wouldn't give up for anything.

"That's fine," Genna scribbled on her notepad. "You're hiring a housekeeper not a grandmother."

"Good." He devoured the muffin, thinking it was the most exquisite thing he'd ever tasted—next to Genna's lips. "These muffins are fabulous."

"Thank you," she said, not looking up.

"And that pie you brought over looks great."

"I'm glad you think so." She continued writing.

Jared watched her, smiling to himself. She had shown up at his kitchen door at eight A.M. sharp, dressed in navy walking shorts, a pink oxford-cloth shirt, and big tortoiseshell reading glasses that made her eyes look impossibly large and guileless. She'd had a notebook under one arm and a wicker basket on the other. He guessed this schoolgirl look was intended to cool his ardor. *Try again, Genna.* If only she knew he was fantasizing making love to her with her wearing nothing but those glasses.

"I think I know someone who might fit the require-ments," she said, thinking of Amy's Aunt Bernice, who lived five blocks away. Bernice had been around. She wouldn't bat an eye at Jared's . . . uniqueness. "I'll call her and see if she's interested and if she can come by for an interview."

She made more notes, mainly to keep her wayward

gaze off Jared. He'd answered the door wearing nothing but a red velvet bathrobe and a pair of gray wool socks. The robe gaped open now, exposing a wide expanse of muscular hair-covered chest. He didn't seem to care. She was sure he would have felt just as comfortable sitting there stark naked.

That thought suffused her body with heat. It was too easy to remember the feel of his fabulous body against hers and too hard to remember he wasn't her type. Oh, why in the world had she ever let him kiss her? She hooked a finger inside the collar of her blouse and swallowed hard.

"While I'm on the phone," she said a bit raggedly, "you can put some clothes on and go mow the lawn."

He chuckled deviously, an unholy gleam in his eye. "Don't you like my outfit, Genna?"

"It isn't exactly haute couture for lawn mowing," she said dryly, arching a delicate brow at him.

Jared leaned across the table, forcing her to look into his twinkling eyes. "I love it when you talk French to me, Gen. Do it again."

She leveled a no-nonsense look at him. "Mow the lawn, Jared."

"Okay," he said equably, sitting back in his chair. "Plaid this time?"

"Regular."

He frowned. "As in plain?"

"Plain. Nondescript."

"Herringbone?" His brows lifted in a show of hope.

"Plain, ordinary, free from affectation, unremarkable." She didn't let his scowl daunt her. "Normal people don't mow their lawns in patterns. And get rid of the flamingos."

Suddenly he looked like a little boy who'd been told Christmas had been canceled and he could never have a puppy or join the Cub Scouts. Genna felt her resolve sway.

"All of them?" he asked.

Darn it, yes, she said to herself. She hated those cheap plastic vultures; they were eyesores. But Jared looked so genuinely disappointed. *Be tough with him, Genna. Steel yourself.*

"I kind of like them," he said sadly.

The steel cracked and crumbled like old plaster. "All right, you can keep two—"

"Six."

"Four. Two in front and two in back."

"Done."

He stood up and demonstrated some respect for Genna's sensibilities by tightening the belt of his robe. The action didn't keep her from thinking that red was an incredibly sexy color on him and that it brought out his tanned good looks. She was going to stop thinking things like that as soon as he left the room, she told herself. But instead of leaving, he came toward her, leaned down, and kissed her.

"We're gonna be a great team, Genna," he said against her lips. "Trust me. I know these things."

Trust him? When pigs fly.

He sauntered out of the kitchen singing something about being in heaven and walking on clouds.

He even sings sexily, she thought.

With Jared out mowing the lawn and Alyssa across the street playing with Courtney Dennison, Genna took a tour of the house, making decorating notes. She had feared it would resemble a frat house, but it wasn't so bad. Jared had more or less left it alone, thank God.

The basement had been turned into a miniature gym with shiny, chrome-plated Nautilus machines. The big country kitchen had been left completely unadorned except for a giant pink hippopotamus cookie jar filled with dry, unappetizing, storebought cookies. She made a note to bring over some of the peanut butter–chocolate chunk cookies she'd baked at one A.M.

Crayon pictures Alyssa had drawn covered the front of the refrigerator. They would definitely stay. Genna smiled. Each one depicted a very tall stick person, Jared. She recognized him by his hair and earring. Some showed their new house, and most had Flurry in them somewhere. One showed "Uncle Brutus" with his Mohawk hairdo. There was even one that immortalized Genna. Her head looked like a pyramid, and she had lopsided breasts and a chocolate chip cookie in each hand.

A print of dogs playing poker hung in the formal dining room. Genna grimaced. That would have to go. An eighteenth-century watercolor should hang on the rich cream and navy wallpaper, she decided. A beautiful cherry corner cabinet stood empty. She had a set of china that would look perfect in it. Maybe she would loan it to him.

The living room held large, comfortable-looking masculine furniture covered in a nubby oatmeal fabric. The arrangement was haphazard. A minor problem. A framed poster of the Hartford Hawks logo was the only wall decoration. A dozen football trophies sat on the oak mantel in no kind of order.

Throw pillows would give the room color, she noted on her pad. Maybe they could group the football stuff around Jared's desk, an oak rolltop beauty that sat off to the far side of the door, cluttered with papers.

She looked around, wondering what to do with the walls. She had suggested hiring a decorator for the house, but Jared had refused. It was important to him that his house look like a homey, lived-in home rather than a layout for *House Beautiful*. That made sense.

Genna glanced out the window to make sure Jared wasn't doing the lawn in paisley. She shook her head. He wore faded cutoffs that strained the bounds of decency and an enormous Chinese coolie hat. She printed the word *wardrobe* on her legal pad.

Sliding down onto the window seat, she wondered what his lawyer would have to say when he called back. Could his sister-in-law really try to take Alyssa away? The possibility made Genna sick. She freely admitted the shy little girl had stolen her heart. She hated to think of not having Alyssa around. And if it bothered her so much, what must it be doing to Jared? she wondered.

Not fit to be a parent. Anger boiled inside Genna. Jared was a little unorthodox, but he was more fit to be a parent than many so-called normal people she knew.

He went by the window again with a flamingo dangling by its throat from a belt loop on his shorts.

Genna shook her head. "Now I'm defending him."

She tried to imagine the sister-in-law, Simone. Jared's comments made the woman sound like the next prime-time soap vixen: Alexis Colby in a bad mood. It was hard to picture her in a different light, since Genna was on Jared's side, but she made an effort. Natasha from *Rocky and Bullwinkle* was as good as it got. Women who tried to take children away from their natural fathers just couldn't be pictured as Beaver Cleaver's mom.

Of course, Genna thought, Simone didn't look at Jared and see Robert Young from *Father Knows Best* either. Her perceptions of him would have been colored by his divorce from Elaine. And Simone had lost her only sister. It was probably natural for her to want to have Alyssa fill that void in her life.

Genna glanced back out at Jared, who was trying to push the lawn mower while the puppy bit into his sneaker and pulled in the opposite direction. Even though she hadn't known him long and still refused to admit she liked him, she already felt an intense loyalty toward him. Simone could rot. Genna would do everything she could think of to help Jared.

Bernice was the ideal housekeeper for J. J. Hennessy. Fifty-nine, and built like the corner mailbox with a poof of red hair, her personality was just a little left of center. After spending her entire life in Brooklyn working in an underarm deodorant factory, she had retired and divorced at fifty-five and moved to Tory Hills to be near her favorite niece. Bernice was gruff and outspoken, but she had a heart of gold and more sense than to feed a five-year-old sausage-anchovy pizza.

It took all of ten minutes for Jared to hire her. Bernice fell in love with Alyssa on sight, though she readily agreed to Jared's terms of noninterference where his daughter was concerned. There was a token argument over salary, then Bernice said, "Okay, boss," and padded off in her Nikes to start the laundry.

"I love that woman." Jared beamed. "Did you hear what she called me?"

"Don't let it go to your head, Hennessy."
"Will you call me boss, Gen?"
"Start moving the furniture, Jared."

Genna sat at her kitchen counter that evening, making out a grocery list while she waited for the timer to go off so she could take the double fudge brownies out of the oven and put the German chocolate cake in.

"I am not upset," she said aloud as she tried to think of people to give the goodies to. Was that rest home bake sale this weekend?

"Perfect," she said to herself. "Take all this food up there and then check yourself in, Genna."

She may or may not have been upset, but one thing was clear—she was spending more on baking supplies than she was making on this so-called job. She looked over her list and tried to eliminate items.

It was all J.J.'s fault. He had her bouncing off the walls with his sexy body, sultry kisses, and outrageous behavior. He was driving her crazy. One minute she was swearing up and down she didn't like him, the next she was exhibiting all the symptoms of malaria just because he'd looked at her a certain way. How could it be possible to want to kiss him and slap that teasing grin off his face all at the same time?

"He's not for you, Genna," she said. *And why do you have to remind yourself if you don't like him?*

The back door banged.

"Hey, Teach, what's cooking?"

She scowled at him over her shoulder. "Don't you ever knock?"

"Only when I run on cheap gas." He straddled the stool next to hers, picked three oranges out of her fruit bowl, and started juggling. "Come on, Gen, let's go. It's singles' night at Fred's Foodtown."

"Please," she drawled with annoyance. "I will not go shopping for a man like I would for a—a—a leg of lamb." She added leg of lamb to the list in front of her.

"Oh, come on. It'll be fun. We can pretend we don't know each other."

"Don't tempt me."

He caught all the oranges and clutched them to his chest, gazing dreamily into space. "We may by chance bump into each other by the meat counter. I can see it all: I'm standing near the chicken, fondling the breasts. Then I move on to the beef, eyeing your rump roast while you gaze raptly at my tenderloins."

"You're perverted," she said evenly, scribbling steak on her list.

"Who knows?" He put the oranges down and draped an arm across her shoulders. "Maybe we'll find love near the bathroom tissue as we dance cheek to cheek and squeeze each other's Charmin."

Worn down to the point of no control, Genna started to giggle, then laugh outright. Shaking her head, she gasped a breath and said, "Don't."

"Don't what?" Jared asked.

"Don't make me laugh!" she said, laughing, sliding off the stool and going to the stove to take out the brownies. She had to hold her stomach with one hand and maneuver the pan with the other.

"Why not?"

"Because. I'm liable to forget I don't like you."

His voice softened. "Would that be so bad?"

Genna sobered, put the pan on the stove, and turned to face him. She sighed. "I'm afraid so. You're not what I need."

Jared slid off the stool and closed the distance between them. His pride didn't smart even a little bit. Genna liked him all right, he was sure of that. She didn't like liking him, but she did just the same. His blue eyes looked deep into hers as he took the oven mitt off her hand and caressed her cheek with it. "What about what you *want?*"

The texture of his voice ran over her, both rough and smooth, like raw silk. He's standing too close, she thought. His warm, hard body beckoned hers. She could never think straight when he got close. It was as if he radiated some kind of magnetic field that made all her mental instruments go haywire. And those incredible eyes of his didn't help any either. She forced her eyes shut to close out their hypnotic beauty.

"I want . . ." Her voice was thin and flimsy, like chiffon. She tried again, "I want stability, security—"

"Invest in CDs. Life was meant for living, Genna. Grab it while you've got the chance."

She took a step back from him and opened her eyes, feeling more in control. "You're not what I want. You're a crazy person."

"Hey, look out!" He winced, a smile teasing his mouth. "You'll bruise my ego."

"Baloney. You've got an ego the size of the Empire State building."

He grinned and leered at her. "Yeah, and you should see the rest of me."

Genna slanted him a disgusted look and fell onto the gold-tiled floor in a fit of laughing. Jared joined her, leaning back against a cupboard and stretching his long, muscular legs out in front of him. Dragging herself to a sitting position beside him, Genna struggled for control, finally clearing her throat and taking a deep breath as she wiped tears from her face with a hotpad.

"So, where's Alyssa?"

"At the movies with Courtney and Amy. *Cinderella*. I would have gone, too, but those ugly stepsisters give me the creeps. He arched up to fish in the pocket of his jeans, leaning into Genna as he did so, and pulled out a crumpled package of M&M's. He poured several into her palm, then poured some directly into his mouth. Munching on them, he asked, "So what have you got against crazy people?"

Genna singled out a yellow M&M and popped it into her mouth. "My father was a crazy person. He worked as a boiler maintenance man, but he thought of himself as an inventor."

"Oh, yeah? What'd he invent?"

"The personal portable inflatable dome for all-weather yard parties, among other equally absurd things."

"Don't think I've ever seen one."

"Nor are you likely to," Genna said, the old bitterness

sneaking up on her. "He was an irresponsible dreamer. He spent all his time goofing off with his ridiculous inventions. They never sold. One day he was carrying boxes of the useless junk up to the attic, and he had a heart attack and died."

"I'm sorry," Jared said quietly, watching her struggle with some deep inner emotion.

"Yeah, well, no great loss," Genna mumbled, fighting off the feelings of helplessness and anger the memory conjured up. "He left my mother with three daughters to raise and not a penny in insurance."

"What'd you do?"

Staring at the cupboards across from them, she didn't answer right away. Finally she just said, "We got by."

She didn't want to tell him about the lean years that had followed her father's death, the years before her mother had met and married Bob Hastings. Bob was a brick. He'd given them all a nice safe home, security, and love. He was an insurance underwriter, the kind of man a woman could depend on.

They just sat for a while, Jared mulling her story over in his head. No wonder she was so hung up on her Mr. Right being normal with a boring job. Those things equaled security to her, the security she had never had as a child.

Jared thought of himself as an individual, a good euphemism for being a little off the wall. And he had an unusual career, a career he was envied and admired for, but one the average kindergarten teacher—Genna in particular—was probably threatened by.

Based on what her father had done, Genna had convinced herself that Jared's individuality meant irresponsibility. She'd taken one look at his diamond earring and stamped him as Mr. Wrong. He intended to show her over the next few weeks that looks often were deceiving. He was as reliable as Old Faithful. Given a little time, he hoped she'd see that.

Genna got up, padded to a cupboard and took out wineglasses, then to the refrigerator, where she removed a bottle of white wine. These she handed down to Jared. She grabbed the container of apple cookies and brought it down to the floor with her.

"So," she asked as he poured the wine, "is your whole family as weird as you are?"

"Yep," he said, grinning as he handed her a glass. "My dad designs twelve-meter racing yachts and builds fireworks in the garage in his spare time. My mother teaches theater at DePaul University. She speaks fluent Gaelic and once decorated each room in our house to look like the set of a different Shakespearean play."

As they drank the wine and ate cookies, Jared told Genna about growing up in a big family where everyone was encouraged to be themselves. He told her all about his three brothers and three sisters—he was number four in the group. He'd gone to college at Notre Dame, where he'd majored in partying and minored in chasing women. He'd come away with a degree in mass communications and a permanent knot on his head where one of the retired priests had whacked him with a crucifix for fooling around during Mass.

Genna listened, a relaxed smile on her face. Amy had told her Jared had been the most sought after high school player in the country and that he'd won the Heisman trophy his senior year of college. He'd taken over as quarterback of the Hawks his second year as a pro. The team had been on the bottom of the heap, but he'd stuck it out with them as they rebuilt into a championship team.

Jared mentioned none of these things, and Genna began to wonder how she could have thought him arrogant. Sure he'd come across the day they'd met like he'd believed his T-shirt slogan about being God's gift to women, but she was learning that was an act of sorts. He kidded around as if he were the most obnoxious man on earth, but when it counted, he was quiet and thoughtful.

She studied him surreptitiously as he refilled their glasses, that now-familiar electric sensation zipping through her, mingling with the tingling warmth of wine in her belly. He was one incredibly sexy hunk of a guy. There was no denying that. She felt more and more attracted to him. There was no denying that either.

"Where on earth do you get those T-shirts?" she asked, staring at the red cotton top stretched across his mile-wide chest. Two black lobsters held up a sign that read EAT PETE'S SEAFOOD. HE NEEDS THE MONEY.

The corners of his mouth turned up. "Fans send them. It's kind of a tradition."

"You really don't go out hunting for them?"

He laughed at the relief in her voice, sensing a barrier going down between them. "No, but I like them and I feel obligated to wear them."

"That's sweet," Genna said, genuinely touched. He was a star, he didn't need to play to the whimsy of fans. He could have thrown the things in a box—he still would have been a star. But he wore them in honor of the people who supported him.

"Oh, yeah?" he said, setting his glass aside and taking Genna's from her. He shifted onto one hip and leaned so close, Genna's eyes almost crossed looking at his short Irish nose. "Well, I think *you're* sweet."

His mouth closed over hers, warm and gentle, seeking, tasting. Genna sighed into his mouth as his kiss coaxed her lips apart and his tongue delved in to sample the flavor of desire. Her hand came up to rest along his jaw, the shadow of his beard rasping pleasantly against her palm.

"Mmmm . . ." he murmured, pressing tiny kisses to the very corners of her mouth. "You *are* sweet."

Genna could barely breathe, she was so startled at the sensations taking over her body. When he touched her, she lost all control of herself. She felt boneless as she leaned into him, initiating the kiss herself this time. A shudder ran through her at Jared's moan of pleasure when she pressed her tongue into his mouth to explore. He tasted wonderfully of chocolate and wine and apple cookies.

In one smooth move Jared pulled her onto his lap, never breaking the kiss. One hand sank into her thick hair, the other strayed under her navy polo shirt, his fingertips feather-stroking their way up her rib cage to the swell of her breast. He cupped the soft, heavy flesh, his thumb caressing the tight bud at its center.

Her mind a mist of passion, Genna gasped into his mouth and arched against him, her thigh pressing hard against his arousal. Deep inside her an exquisite, empty ache throbbed, begging her to let go the last shreds of her sanity. Jared could assuage that ache. Never mind that she hadn't been with a man in nearly a year. Never mind that she hardly knew this one and would have sworn up and down in a saner moment that she could hardly tolerate the sight of him. There was something in his touch, in his kiss that scattered all logic and cut down to the plain unvarnished truth: she wanted him.

Jared was thinking along the same lines. He wanted to lay Genna down and gently tug her top out of his way so he could see her breasts, touch and kiss them. He wanted to ease her white shorts down her legs so he could bury himself between them.

But even as Genna's hands slid under his T-shirt to caress his back, Jared was acutely aware of one major fact: they were making out on her kitchen floor. Not that he minded. It just wasn't the right place for their first time together. And, although his hormones were willing to put up a lively argument, it was too soon.

He eased his hand from the sweet fullness of her breast, ignoring her whimpered protest, and brought it up to rest against her cheek as he lifted his lips from hers.

"You have a very sexy mouth," he said, his voice warm and textured like velvet.

"Really?" The word was whispered through her wet lips.

"No one's ever told you that?" He kissed her earlobe.

"Uh-uh."

"A testimony to the sad quality of the men in your life." He kissed the tip of her upturned nose. "Your mouth is very, very sexy."

Genna sighed as his lips touched hers. His tongue ever so gently traced the outline of her mouth.

"I like the way this corner kicks up all by itself right before you make a smart remark." He pressed a kiss to the right corner of her mouth. "And I love this bottom lip when you pout."

"I don't pout," she stated.

He chuckled, a deep, hoarse, masculine rumbling low in his throat. "There it is." He took her lower lip between his and sucked gently, then pulled back away from her.

He stared into Genna's eyes, and he waited for the other shoe to drop. Any second now she was going to start to feel guilty, he was sure of it. Instead, she started to giggle.

"I think we've had too much wine."

"Naw." He smiled, relieved. He rested his forehead against hers. "Not quite. I'm sober enough to know that if I got you to drink a little more, I could call a blitz and rush your pass defense."

"What would happen then?" she asked, her voice a husky purr she didn't even recognize.

"Sack."

"Sack the quarterback? But you're the quarterback."

"Yeah," he said, grinning lazily. "In this game sacking the quarterback takes on a whole new meaning."

"I see," she said with a low chuckle. A pleasantly languid sensation of anticipation ambled over her. "So are you going to ply me with liquor?"

"Nope."

A mixture of disappointment and embarrassment flushed Genna's cheeks as Jared helped her up from the floor. He probably thought she was desperate and wanted him to get her drunk and make love to her on the ceramic tile. Her aching body told her he wasn't far from wrong.

Jared brushed her hair out of her eyes and gave her a tender smile. "When we make love I want us both sober. Makes for a better memory and a lot less guilt."

"Well," she said, pretending to be in a huff, her nose in the air. "You're not my type anyway."

He chuckled and tweaked her cheek. "Sure, Gen, just like you're not my type."

"I'm not," she said reasonably.

"We'll see."

The sound of a car pulling up to the curb came through the screen door.

"That's probably Amy with Alyssa," Jared said, checking the thin gold watch on his wrist. "I'd better go."

Genna wanted to say something to him about what had happened between them, but her brain was jumbled with words that wouldn't sort into any kind of order. What was one supposed to say to a man after a romantic interlude on the kitchen floor?

Jared smiled down at her knowing she was confused. She'd come right out and said she didn't like him, didn't want him, then turned to Play-Doh in his arms. He gave her a wink. "See ya at school tomorrow, Teach."

Genna leaned against the doorjamb as she watched him cross her yard and his and scooped his daughter up into his arms when he reached the front sidewalk. There was a hell of a lot more to that man than punk hair and a Jack Nicholson grin.

She had to admit he was fun to be with. Unsettling, but fun. And he kissed like a thief. He'd stolen every ounce of strength and willpower from her so she had to prop herself up in the doorway, or melt into a puddle on the kitchen floor.

What did it all mean?

Life was meant for living, Genna.

Have a summer fling.

That seemed to be what he was thinking too. Modern adults did that sort of thing all the time, she reminded herself. He didn't have to be Mr. Right for her to have fun with him. She could have a relationship with a man without thinking how his name would look engraved on a wedding invitation, couldn't she?

"He's still not for you, Genna," her mouth said, but her brain wasn't convinced so easily anymore.

Five

"Before I come in I want to make one thing perfectly clear," Amy announced through Genna's screen door. "You are *not* sending any food home with me. I've gained five pounds since J.J. moved in. I don't see why *your* anxieties should go to *my* hips."

"I don't have any anxieties," Genna insisted as she dribbled icing on a pound cake.

"Oh, really?" Amy let herself in. She poured a cup of coffee and sat down at the dining room table. "What are you trying to do then, put Torino's Bakery out of business single-handedly?"

"I don't know what you mean."

"I mean," Amy droned on, "no one in the neighborhood has had to turn on their oven since you came back from vacation. And let me ask you this, why haven't *you* gained any weight? What are you, a space alien?"

"I'm ignoring you, Amy."

"I'm calling the *Enquirer*. 'My Neighbor Is a Space Alien.' " Her hand blocked out the imaginary headline in front of her.

Genna calmly brought her coffee cup to the table and sat down with a saccharine smile. "And how are you today, Amy?"

"Don't think I didn't see Jared Hennessy leave your house last night, because I did." She pinned Genna with a look that had compelled more than one errant child to spill the beans. Her brown eyes narrowed and her little mouth puckered up. Color flushed her pudgy cheeks.

"Did you?" Genna's face was the picture of innocence. She sipped her coffee. "How was the movie?"

"The same as it was the last five times I took kids to see it." Against her will, Amy's gaze wandered to a plate of nut bread to her left. She drummed her fingers on the table. "J.J.'s little girl is a doll."

Genna smiled as she felt a strange stirring in her heart. "She is, isn't she? Something in those big blue eyes makes my heart flip over when I look at her." She'd always wanted a little girl of her own. She might have had a daughter like Alyssa if things had worked out differently with Allan. But they hadn't.

"She's so shy," Amy said. "I try to draw her out, but only Jared seems to be able to do that. He's so good with her."

"It's been hard on her," Genna said, frowning. "Losing her mother, moving to a new town."

"Yeah, it's going to be even harder on her if that rotten aunt takes her away."

"How'd you hear about that?" Genna asked, concerned that the news had somehow hit the neighborhood grapevine.

Amy snatched a piece of nut bread and put it on the table in front of her. "The all-knowing, all-seeing Aunt Bernice. Don't worry. Jared told her, and she wouldn't tell anyone but me, and I wouldn't tell anyone but you, and you already know. Do you think his sister-in-law can pull it off?"

A worried frown creased Genna's brow. "Jared's lawyer says she can try. Even though Jared and his ex-wife had joint custody, it seems Elaine named her sister as guardian of Alyssa if anything ever happened to her. That complicates things. Plus, Jared has a wild reputation. Whether it's deserved or not may not matter. If Simone gets a judge who's sympathetic to her argument and if she has some evidence that makes Jared look bad . . ."

Amy shook her head. "You'd think it'd be all cut and dried. I mean, Jared is Alyssa's father, there shouldn't be any question about custody."

They drank their coffee and listened to the birdsong drifting in on the summer-scented air. Finally needing to break the silence and her train of thought, Genna said. "I suppose you know about my 'job' too."

"Of course. I see you got him to cut down on the flamingo population. Good girl."

"I didn't have the heart to make him get rid of all of them."

Willpower crumbling, Amy popped the nut bread into her mouth and chewed. Smiling, she waved an accusatory finger at her friend and singsonged in her distinctly unmusical voice, "You're softening up on him, Genna."

"I am not," she denied, her eyes looking everywhere but at the kitchen floor.

"You have to admit he's charming."

Genna scowled in grudging admission. "I suppose he's charming . . . in an obnoxious sort of way."

The back door banged.

Singing to himself that he'd had his eye on a certain lady for days, Jared danced in and boogied his way across the kitchen to the counter. He started taking cookies out of the cookie jar and slipping them into the many pockets of his camouflage paratrooper pants. Spotting the ladies, he shoved his sunglasses back on his head and leaned his elbows on the counter. His smile moseyed across his face, setting Genna's skin a-tingle. His gaze captured hers. "Good morning, Amy. *Good morning, Genna.*"

How was it her name sounded so much longer when he said it? And *so* much sexier.

"Morning, J.J.," Amy said, her amused expression directed at Genna. "What'd you learn in school yesterday, J.J.?"

Jared grinned, coming around the counter. Genna swallowed hard. He wore a black tank top as if it were a second skin. It made his shoulders look impossibly wide.

"Oh, I learned all kinds of stuff. I learned how to mow the lawn and how to arrange furniture." He slid down onto the chair at the head of the table, resting his tanned forearms on the smooth cherry wood. "Thursday is double coupon day at Fred's. Never make a pass at the Avon lady. A shirt and tie is acceptable dress at a PTA meeting. I guess pants are optional."

Amy burst into a fit of giggles that sounded like machine-gun fire.

Jared's gaze fell on Genna. "But my favorite lesson was 'All About Kitchen Tile.' "

The insinuation went right by Amy, as intended, but Genna flushed scarlet.

"Genna's an excellent teacher," he went on, straight-faced.

"Yeah," Amy agreed. "All the kids really like her."

"I like her," he said silkily, his eyes smoldering, "and I'm a big boy."

Genna turned three shades darker than scarlet. She was going to kill him—one handsome inch at a time.

She stood up suddenly with murder in her eyes and shoved the plate of nut bread at Amy. "There's your nut bread, Amy. Thanks for stopping by," she said loudly.

Amy's brows puckered together in confusion. She'd obviously missed something. "But Genna," she whined. "I don't want nut bread. I have to go to Weight Watchers today."

"Take it with you." Genna smiled unpleasantly. "You can share it."

"All right already!" Snatching the plate from her friend's hands, she gave Jared a brief salute and backed toward the door.

"PMS," Jared said affably.

Amy nodded, slipping outside.

Genna treated Jared to her most baleful glare. "I do not have PMS."

She turned on her heel and limped to the kitchen, where she began noisily rummaging through drawers. Jared ambled in, crossing his arms over his chest as he leaned back against the counter.

"What ya lookin' for, Teach?"

"The meanest, wickedest-looking knife I own," she said between clenched teeth.

"What for?"

"For to kill you with."

"Corporal punishment is against the law in Connecticut."

She turned on him, smacking him on his flat stomach with a spaghetti spoon. "*You* should be against the law in Connecticut!"

"Me!" he blurted out incredulously. "What'd I do?"

Staring disbelievingly at his wounded expression, she threw up her hands. "What did you do? What did you do! How could you? How could you say those things with Amy sitting right there?"

He waved it off. "She didn't know what I was talking about."

"That's not the point," Genna said, seething, genuinely upset. They had come dangerously close to making love and he had belittled the experience by joking about it. Now she thought of last night and felt cheap.

"Oh, Genna," Jared said softly, accurately reading her mind. He took the spoon out of her hand and pulled her into his arms, where she stood as stiff as Candy the mannequin. "I'm sorry, honey." He kissed her hair and rubbed her back through her blue-striped blouse. "I wasn't making fun of last night."

He tipped her head back and settled his lips against hers, feeling them go unwillingly from unyielding to pliant. She tasted deliciously of coffee and nut bread and Genna.

"I just had to tease you a little." He smiled mischievously and kissed the tip of her upturned nose.

"Why?" she asked, hurt and anger evident in her tone.

" 'Cause I love it when you turn burgundy."

Her anger sputtered and died, and exasperated humor bubbled up inside her. She shook her head. "What am I going to do with you?"

He quirked one eyebrow, a dangerous gleam in his eye. "You're open to suggestions?"

"I don't need suggestions, I have plenty of ideas. And none of them are what you're thinking," she told him as she backed out of his embrace. She went to the counter to start returning to their drawer the utensils she'd thrown around.

Jared fell back into place beside her, nibbling on the earpiece of his sunglasses he watched her thoughtfully. "Personally, I believe a relationship should receive input from both parties—or *all* parties if you're into that."

"That's a lovely thought. Of course, since we don't have a relationship—except in the business sense—it's irrelevant." I'm giving myself a way out before it's too late, Genna thought. But somehow she knew, had this fatalistic feeling, she wasn't going to take it.

Jared shut the drawer with a bump of his hip, turned Genna, and pinned her against the counter all in one move. His brows slashed down angrily, but there was that familiar twinkle of laughter in his eyes.

"So you think you can just toy with me on your kitchen floor, and then cast me aside like—like—yesterday's fish?"

Genna made a disgusted face at his analogy and tried to squirm out of her tight spot, but Jared wouldn't let her budge. Iron-muscled arms blocked escape on either side, and she was held firmly in the V of his legs, a thigh on either side of hers so thick and hard, they may as well have been tree trunks. He leaned forward, bending her back as she tried to avoid breast-to-chest contact. He was so magnificently, aggressively male, a shimmering shiver of excitement rippled over Genna from head to toe. Her scalp tingled, her nipples hardened. Another fraction of an inch and the aching points would rub against the solid wall of his chest.

"*I* think we have a relationship," Jared said, knowing he was taking a risk by pushing her. To soften the statement, he added, "Of sorts."

Clinging tenaciously to a ragged remnant of common sense, Genna said, "How can we? We don't have anything in common."

"Sure we do," he said, lowering his head to nibble at

her earlobe. "We have each other. Mmmm. That's the most important thing."

Genna's head was starting to swim, swirling with thoughts of running her hands up his back and arching against him like a wanton feline. She had to get a grip on herself before she started groping Jared. But how could she get away from him? He was about as easy to move as a stalled bus.

Abandoning the idea of sheer brute force, she opted for a sneak attack of tickles to the ribs. Well-placed, nimble fingers had him doubled over instantly, screaming, "Personal foul! Roughing the quarterback!"

Ducking the arm he swung out to catch her, Genna grabbed a dishtowel for protection and twirled it in a menacing manner. "Don't come any closer," she cautioned, backing toward the refrigerator. "I warn you, I can snap this thing with deadly accuracy."

To prove her point, she flicked her wrist, cracking the towel a hairbreadth from Jared's flat belly, effectively halting his advance. He took a step back and dropped his hands to his hips.

"Now," Genna said, returning to the subject with a clear head, "I'll admit to a certain . . . physical . . . attraction—"

Jared's eyes lit up like blue neon signs.

"But people need more than that to base a relationship on. Look at us. We couldn't be more different."

"Variety," he argued.

"Common ground," she parried.

"We have lots of things in common!" Jared said.

Genna arched a skeptical brow. "Such as?"

"A—a—you like to cook, I like to eat. You like to sun, I like to watch you."

She rolled her eyes. "Yeah, we're practically peas in a pod."

Jared shifted on his feet, inching closer to Genna, his mind automatically sifting through play options to decide how best to get her in his arms. He much preferred the way her mind worked when her body was pressed to his. "Haven't you ever heard that opposites attract?"

Genna caught his movement and twitched the dish-towel. "Freeze, turkey, or you'll be sporting matching belly buttons."

Jared faked to the right then bolted left, grabbing the towel as she cracked it and reeling her in with a jerk of his arm so that she thudded into his chest. He wasted no time wrapping his arms around her.

"See," he said with a lazy grin. "Like magnets."

"Poles apart," she insisted, trying not to breathe in his warm male scent, trying to block out the feel of the blatantly male anatomy molded against her.

"Look, Gen," he said, choosing his words carefully so he wouldn't scare her off, "you're free. I'm free. We're both attracted. We're adults. Where's the harm in giving it a shot?"

Where's the harm? Hadn't she been thinking the same thoughts last night? Now, as then, she couldn't come up with any good answers. He was right, she didn't have any hot prospects for romance. She'd be all right with Jared as long as they kept things light. It wouldn't do for her to fall in love with him, because it wouldn't work out on a long-term basis—certainly he wasn't even interested on that level. But of course she wasn't in any real danger of falling in love with him anyway. Heaven knew she wasn't even sure she liked him.

Jared watched Genna's face as conflicting emotions seemed to war within her and he waited for her to comment. She seemed to be considering his offer of a light romance. Maybe if he reassured her of her freedom she'd be more inclined to accept.

"I'm talking light romance here. We'll have fun together. Nothing heavy. No pressure. We'll date. No strings attached."

Fun. No strings. That was what she'd been thinking too. So why did it sting a little bit when he said it? Pride, she told herself. It just pricked her vanity a little to have him say he wasn't even considering a serious involvement. Silly, she thought, since I'm definitely not considering it either.

"Light romance?" she asked, leaning back in his arms so she had a good view of his face.

She was definitely thinking about it. He smiled and crossed his fingers behind her back for good luck. "All the fun and a third less calories. What better way to spend the summer?" Once she saw what a good guy he was, he hoped, maybe she'd consider extending the contract.

"Well . . . okay," Genna gave in, as she'd known all along she would. She pried her left arm out from between them and checked her watch, then glanced at Jared's wild black hair. "The only date you need to worry about now is the one I made for you with the barber. If we don't get going, we'll be late."

"You don't like my haircut?" His eyes glittered as he ran a hand over the ebony spikes.

"It looks as if rodents chewed it off as you slept," Genna said dryly.

"Well, don't tell Brutus, you'll hurt his feelings."

"You let Brutus style your hair?" The thought of that man loose with a scissors in his hand was enough to make her blood run cold.

"Honey," Jared laughed. "I let Brutus do whatever he wants."

Jared, Genna, and Alyssa all trooped down to Gorgeous Guy's Hair Emporium on Tory Hills's Old Market Street, where the brick buildings dated back to before the Revolution. When they came out half an hour later, Jared looked more like a *GQ* model than a rock star.

Guy very cleverly had left the top short and had cut off the long strands that had straggled down Jared's neck. The style left him looking amazingly clean-cut, and Genna's fingers were itching to run up and down the back of his smooth, strong neck. Even Alyssa liked the new look, proclaiming her daddy to be "very pretty."

"Clothes make the man," Genna proclaimed, dragging Jared by the arm from Gorgeous Guy's toward Wagnall's Clothiers, the one and only men's shop in Tory Hills. They wouldn't be able to outfit Jared totally here, but at least he could get a couple of shirts that didn't qualify as walking billboards.

Jared balked, eyeing the nattily dressed mannequins in the window with obvious distaste. "I already have clothes."

Genna let go of his hand and planted her hands on her hips. She looked up and down at the black tank top and camouflage pants he wore. "Yeah, you're all set if we want to go out to eat in the jungles of Nicaragua." She gave Alyssa a wink and a grin. "Come on, Lyss, grab Daddy's hand and let's drag him in here."

Alyssa giggled and immediately began tugging on her father's hand, jumping up and down and pulling at him. "Come *on*, Daddy!"

With the help of a clerk who held the door open, they managed to get Jared into the store. He was still scowling when they came back out with two button-down oxford shirts, a plain navy blue tie, two polo shirts, and a pair of navy gabardine trousers.

"Cheer up," Genna said. "It's good for your new image to be seen shopping in the local stores. Besides, now you won't have to worry about taking me out to dinner at a nice restaurant and having them punish you by making you wear one of those awful ties they keep at the desk for people who underdress."

Jared didn't mention that he had a whole closet full of shirts and ties, since it so obviously pleased Genna to dress him up like a Ken doll. Her picking on him about his everyday clothes irked him a little though, and he got back at her that evening by making choking noises over dinner at Leonie's while tugging at the knot in his new tie.

The next few days were spent schooling Jared on normal, small-town behavior and trying to get him to give up his earring. That was something he flatly refused to do, as the diamond stud had been a gift from his mother. Evenings were devoted to dates that often included Alyssa. They did every normal thing Jared could think of. They went to the movies and to dinner. They even played miniature golf.

Everywhere they went Jared was pestered for autographs. Genna watched him closely as he signed scraps of paper, always smiling, even when a fan interrupted a meal. She also noticed that many of his fans were women. He attracted them like metal filings to a magnet. It was disgusting. Women of all ages fell willingly under the spell of his unusual charm. More than one woman had made it clear that she would fall under more than that if he were interested, but Jared always turned the ladies away with a wink and a grin.

Wednesday of the following week the three of them piled into Jared's new Mercedes station wagon and headed for downtown Hartford. Jared had agreed to take Genna shopping for accessories for his house and had promised Alyssa a picnic as soon as he took care of "a little something."

His "little something" turned out to be shooting a thirty-second commercial for the NFL's antidrug campaign. Genna and Alyssa were allowed to sit off-camera and watch as makeup people, lighting people, sound technicians, and cameramen fussed over and around Jared. Through all the commotion he remained his amiable self, talking football with the crew and signing autographs. When the director shouted "Action," Jared simply looked directly into the camera and delivered his lines like a pro.

They did three takes, though Genna would have sworn only one had been necessary. She was more than a little surprised at Jared's professional attitude in front of the camera. The way he had talked about his college days and his degree in communications, he would have had her believe he didn't know a light meter from a lens cap, when obviously he knew a lot more.

His acting ability was nothing to sneeze at either. He was very relaxed in front of the camera. Dressed in jeans and a tight Hawks T-shirt, he casually leaned back against a smooth oak desk, his sneakered feet crossed at the ankle, his hands stuffed into his pockets. The wall behind the desk displayed framed photos of Jared in action on the football field, and the shelves held game balls and trophies. When the film started rolling, he looked into the camera as if he were looking into someone's eyes and said his lines as if he were speaking directly to that one person. His message was clear and sincere.

"As quarterback of the Hartford Hawks, I'm known for being a little unorthodox." He grinned engagingly, then grew serious. "But doing my own thing doesn't mean doing drugs. I get my highs on the football field helping my team win championships. I don't need drugs messing that up. Everybody knows drugs are stupid." He gave a harsh laugh. "Why do you think they call it *dope?*"

When Genna asked him why he hadn't mentioned the commercial, he just shrugged it off.

"No big deal," he said, turning his attention to Alyssa. "How'd you like that, muffin?"

Alyssa gave him her shy smile. "Were you on TV, Daddy?"

"I will be." He scooped her up in the crook of his strong arm so they were face-to-face. "They'll run that ad this fall when I'm working."

Alyssa turned to Genna with a proud look. "My daddy plays bootball."

Genna hid her mirth with a smile. After all, she didn't know much more about the sport herself. Jared laughed and kissed his daughter's cheek. "That's *foot*-ball, sweetheart."

Afterward they ate hamburgers in Bushnell Park on the capitol grounds. Every time Genna mentioned shopping, Jared changed the subject. The day was too summer perfect to spend in a store, he'd said. He drove them to Elizabeth Park instead, where they walked through the famous rose gardens and watched people lawn bowling.

The combination of the warm sun and the intoxicating scent of the flowers made Genna feel giddy and weak. She had told herself she could have fun with him without getting her heart involved, but as she watched him lift Alyssa so the little girl could have a better view of the flowers, Genna doubted it.

She'd been attracted to him from the start, but that desire had been easily dampened by her initial low opinion of him. The trouble was, he wasn't Jared the Jerk anymore. He was the Jared who sat on the kitchen floor with her and gently listened to her tale of an unhappy childhood. He was the Jared who forgot little details like winning national awards and making commercials. He was the Jared who always had time for his daughter and his fans. He was the Jared with summer-sky eyes and kisses that stole every scrap of sanity Genna possessed.

She would be a fool to fall for him. He'd never get serious with a kindergarten teacher. And he wasn't the type for her to get serious with either. He'd said himself this was just a summer romance, nothing heavy. It was a convenient relationship that they were both enjoying.

Really, she told herself, there was no reason for her to be afraid of getting overly involved. They were just working together. The boundaries of their arrangement were very clear in her mind: they were working together and they were friends for the summer. Certainly she was adult enough by now to lean over the edge of the waters of romance without falling in.

Of course she was. It had been a long time since she'd been attracted to a man on any level. So now that this major league hunk was showing an interest, she was simply overreacting. She'd gotten too involved in a one-sided romance once before and she was afraid of letting it happen again. That was why she'd hardly even gone out with a man since her breakup with Allan. She knew too well how it hurt to give her heart to someone who wanted only to play handball with it. Allan had left her feeling uncertain of herself as a woman and uncertain of her own judgment. It was only natural that she was skittish of the same thing happening again. But it wasn't going to. She and Jared had become friends. There was nothing scary about that.

Genna smiled to herself as she watched Jared model a big straw bonnet bedecked with flowers for Alyssa. The vendor stood by her cart laughing and clapping her hands at his antics.

Infatuation. That was all she was feeling. He was a

good-looking man, personable in his own strange way. Infatuation. It certainly wasn't . . . the L word. No. It was simply a normal attraction between two healthy adults who had been spending a lot of time together.

She breathed easier knowing she wasn't in any real danger.

Genna sat next to Jared on the edge of his stone patio watching Alyssa at play in the yard with Flurry. She had finally given up on the shopping idea. They had all been ready to come home after their afternoon in the park. "Any news from your lawyer?" she asked.

Jared shook his head. His eyes never left his daughter as he spoke. "Paul said they made all the initial moves, now they just seem to be waiting around. I don't know what their game plan is, but I don't like it." He raised his shoulders as if he were trying to shrug off his apprehension. "Anyway, we're doing our part, so let's talk about something else."

"Okay," Genna said, honoring his desire to drop the subject. "Why didn't you tell me about the commercial?"

Jared shrugged again and sipped from his can of root beer. "I didn't want to make a big deal of it."

"You do a lot of that kind of thing? Commercials, I mean."

"Some."

He was being shy and modest and she knew it. How sweet. Amy had told her he made megabucks doing commercials for several nationally known products. If he was the arrogant jerk she had first thought him to be, he'd have been bragging about it, trying to impress her.

"I thought Alyssa might get a kick out of watching," he said.

"She did. She's very proud of you, you know." Genna smiled at the blush that spread across his cheekbones. She wriggled her foot as the puppy attacked her shoelaces.

"Come on, Flurry!" Alyssa coaxed, one hand holding firmly on top of her head the wreath of flowers Jared had bought her. With a bright red rubber ball in her other hand, she enticed the puppy away from Genna's shoe.

"Do you get paid for a commercial like the one you did today?" Genna questioned.

He shook his head, his gaze on his daughter, who was squealing as the puppy jumped up on her. "Throw it for him, honey!" he called, then said to Genna, "No. That's a public service. The league pays for production costs, but not for my part. They encourage us to do the spots, but even if they didn't, I'd do it. It's a cause I believe in. A lot of kids look up to me. I consider it my responsibility to set a good example, especially since I have sort of a wild reputation. I mean, I like to see kids having a good time, but I don't want them to get the wrong idea. I don't want to see them get mixed up in that kind of trouble."

Genna thought about what he'd said for a minute as the radio played something romantic in the background. At first glance Jared didn't look like the sort of man parents would want their children to emulate. Jared, with his spiked hair and diamond earring and come-hither grin. But he was a sports hero and he was right—kids would look up to him whether their parents wanted them to or not. He could easily have shrugged off the responsibility, told them to live to party and break all the rules. Instead, he told them to be themselves, but to live right.

Impulsively, she leaned over and kissed his cheek. "You're sweet."

He grinned at her, pushing his sunglasses up so she could get the full impact of his startling blue eyes. "So you keep saying. Tsk, tsk, Genna. You're going to have me thinking I'm the teacher's pet." His grin melted down to a sensuous smile and he spoke in his whiskey-on-the-rocks voice that rasped across Genna's skin like velvet. "But that's okay, I don't have anything against petting."

She gave him a black look and shoved him, sending him rolling on the lawn to be attacked by the puppy.

He scrambled to his feet, wiping puppy kisses off his cheek as Alyssa and Genna laughed.

"You're in big trouble now," he warned, shaking a finger at Genna as Alyssa raced into the house with the puppy at her heels.

"I'm terrified," Genna scoffed, but got to her feet just the same, anticipation making her skin tingle.

"I think I bruised something."

"Your pride?" she offered sarcastically.

He raised one dark brow as his lips twitched upward. "Maybe. Wanna go to my room and see?"

"You're impossible!"

"Naw." Quick as a cat, he grabbed her and started to dance to a funky tune on the radio. "Hard maybe, not impossible."

"Disgusting, definitely." She pretended offense just as she pretended not to notice the provocative sway of his hips so near her own.

He chuckled. "You love it and you know it."

She rolled her eyes at the macho line.

Bernice came out the back door wiping her hands on a dishtowel. "Phone, boss."

"Thanks, Bernice." He winked at Genna and danced into the house, singing in his smoky voice about how right he was for her.

Genna strangled a frustrated scream in her throat and dropped onto a white wrought iron chair across from Bernice.

"He's something, ain't he?" the older woman said, crossing her chubby legs. She wore black stirrup pants with high-top sneakers and an oversize Hawks T-shirt that swallowed up her stocky body. The short sleeves hung past her elbows.

"Something *else*," Genna amended, shaking her head in bewilderment. "I don't know what it is about that man. He unleashes something wild in me. I never know whether I'm going to laugh at him or slug him. Do you know what I mean, Bernice?"

Bernice puffed up her red hair and laughed. "Honey, my ex-husband couldn't unleash the dog, but I read a lot of romances and I'd say you're in love."

Horror-stricken, Genna gasped, "With Jared Hennessy?"

"I don't see Tom Selleck hanging around here."

"In . . . L . . . with Jared Hennessey," she mumbled to herself, shuddering. It wasn't possible. She couldn't even verbalize the word, and she'd just finished telling herself it was only infatuation. She decided she should say it out loud. "No. It's only infatuation."

Bernice laughed until Genna thought she was going to choke. She slapped her knee as tears streamed down her flushed face. Finally her guffaws were reduced to gasps by lack of oxygen. "Oh—oh—that's a—a—good one! Boy, have you got it bad, toots!"

Genna scowled, seeing no humor in the situation at all. "Great."

Six

The L word. How had she let it happen? *Had* she let it happen? Maybe Bernice was wrong. Genna had been trying to convince herself of that for two days. Once again she tried telling herself it was just infatuation. She waited. Nothing. No sense of calm came over her. She didn't feel reassured in the least. In fact, she felt vaguely nauseated. *Oh, Lord, I am in . . . the L word.*

How? How had she let herself fall in . . . L . . . with a man like Jared Hennessy? Only a few days before she would have sworn on a stack of Bibles she couldn't stand the sight of him. Now she was in . . . L . . . with him.

Disastrous, she thought as she went through a rack of little girls' jumpers. They were shopping for clothes for Alyssa because Jared had 'sort of ruined' a lot of her things in the wash a few days before he had hired Bernice.

Nothing good can come from this, she told herself. In a few weeks her job would be over, Jared would head for training camp, and she'd be back teaching school. She would have spent the whole summer in . . . L . . . with the wrong man. She was always off balance with Jared. He made her feel as if she were stuck in a pair of haywire inversion boots. And it was a cinch he wasn't in . . . L . . . with her. Jared was just having fun.

She'd gone and done it again, gotten in over her

head with a man who wasn't interested in a future with her. Not only that, he wasn't even her type. He was unconventional, impetuous, outrageous. She was looking for solid, dependable . . . boring.

Jared studied the determined frown on Genna's face and smiled to himself. *She's coming around, I can feel it.* Bernice had said so, and he was starting to believe it. That Genna wasn't very happy about it didn't faze Jared. He was finally winning her over. Her defenses were wearing down and momentum was on his side. Genna was a woman with a good head on her shoulders; sooner or later she'd admit she'd been wrong about him and give in to his charm. He hoped.

She needed time to get used to the idea. If he pushed her, she'd probably tell him to take a hike. He'd promised her a no-strings romance. He wasn't sure that was what he wanted anymore, but he would have to pretend it was true for a while.

Alyssa singled out a red corduroy jumper and insisted she'd wear it every day forever and ever. After she and Genna returned from the fitting room, and Jared paid for the dress, it was added to the bunch of packages in their shopping bag.

"Can I get a new nightie to wear to Courtney's house tonight, Daddy?" she asked as they came to a row of nightgowns.

A worried frown tugged at Jared's features. He stooped down by his daughter and brushed at her black bangs. "Are you sure you want to stay overnight at Courtney's house, Lyss?"

Alyssa's blue eyes begged as eloquently as her voice. "Yes, Daddy, *please* let me stay. I'm a big girl!"

"I know you are, sweetheart." Jared sighed.

Genna watched the exchange, wondering what the problem was, but not wanting to interfere. Amy had arranged to pick Alyssa up at the shopping mall and then treat the girls to pizza, ending the evening with a sleepover at the Dennisons. The girls had talked of little else for two days.

Finally Jared capitulated, against his better judgment. A white eyelet nightgown with blue satin ribbons was bought and went into the shopping bag.

They started down the wide hall of the shopping center, heading for the fountain where they were to meet Amy. As they strolled past the various shops, Jared casually snuck Genna's hand into his. He smiled at her look of surprise, but held her hand firmly. It just seemed right. Genna held Alyssa's hand on one side and his on the other. The word "family" kept strolling through his head. Good word. He liked it.

After her first nervous glance at Jared, Genna trained her gaze on the stores they passed. This wasn't the first time he'd held her hand, but it was the first time since she'd discovered she was in . . . L . . . with him. A strange, intoxicating excitement began to build inside her. A part of her wanted to bolt while another part wanted to do something entirely different. Tingles raced up her arm.

Memories of the way his hand had felt on her bare breast rushed back to Genna with a reality that almost made her gasp. Inside the lacy confines of her bra her nipples hardened and suddenly became hypersensitive to the fabric rubbing over them, rubbing over them as Jared's calloused thumb had that night in her kitchen. A wave of heat spread through her body.

For heaven's sake, Genna, you're in a shopping mall. Knock it off.

She pushed the erotic thoughts from her mind as they came to a store where she always loved to browse but could never afford to buy. A sultry brunette mannequin in the window wore a gorgeous purple taffeta halter-top dress with a double-tiered skirt and a big candy-box bow at her waist in back. It was the most elegant, extravagant thing Genna had ever seen. Her step faltered ever so slightly.

"See something you like?" Jared questioned, bringing them all to a halt.

"Huh? Er—no," she stammered, feeling silly for even looking at such a dress.

A smile played at Jared's mouth and his eyes crinkled at the corners. "Come on, Gen, fess up. You've got your eye on that dress."

"No." She shook her head, blushing.

His smile widened. "Gen-na."

"Okay," she admitted, raising her hands in a gesture of defeat. "It's pretty."

"Try it on."

"Don't be silly."

"Try it on."

"No. What would I do with a dress like that?"

"Wear it to school!" he said with a grin.

She gave him a look. "If teachers dressed like that, there would be riots in the streets."

"So buy it for fun."

"There's nothing fun in spending two hundred dollars on a dress I'll never wear," she pointed out.

Paying no attention to her logical argument, Jared dragged them all into the store. "Try it on."

"Try it on, Genna," Alyssa chimed in.

J.J. caught the eye of a clerk hovering nearby. He smiled using the full force of his magnetism, and Genna thought the woman was going to swoon. "Don't you think she should try it on?"

"Yes. Definitely," the clerk said breathlessly, her eyes glazing over.

"See?" Jared turned back to Genna.

Genna sent the clerk an anemic smile and whispered to J.J. under her breath, "I think she would have said that no matter what you asked her. Ask her if she'd move to Guam with you."

"Not a chance, honey. If she said yes, you'd hold me to it."

All the women in the store were gravitating toward Jared like flowers to the sun. They all beamed and nodded when he gave them his intimate, teasing little smile and asked if they thought Genna should try on the purple dress. It was positively disgusting. Even a blue-haired old lady was bowled over by his charm. She touched Genna's arm and beamed a smile up at her. "Try it on, honey. It's you."

"See?" Jared said innocently. "It's you."

"It's *you.*" Genna scowled. He pretended not to understand.

Feeling outnumbered, Genna gave in. She took the dress into the fitting room. When she emerged, everyone in the store burst into applause.

Jared's breath caught in his throat. His eyes darkened to pewter as he took in the sight of his adorable, curvy little Genna in the sexy dress. He'd known all along she was a doll, but holy cow! he thought. The taffeta cupped her full breasts lovingly and swirled around the feminine swell of her hips. The bow at the waist called attention to the supple lines of her bare back. It'd be worth every penny if she never wore the dress for anyone but him.

Like a man in a trance, Jared handed his gold credit card to the clerk, never taking his eyes off Genna. His voice was a hoarse, gravely whisper as he said, "Wrap it up."

Genna was still blushing, as they wandered around browsing at whatever took their fancy, after delivering Alyssa to Amy.

"I can't believe you bought that dress."

"Believe it."

"You're going to look pretty silly wearing it."

"I bought it for you."

She ignored that the same way she had tried to ignore the hot look in his eyes when she'd come out of the fitting room. "I suppose Candy the mannequin can wear it."

"I bought it for you."

"I won't wear it."

"You'll wear it." When he turned to grin at her, Genna stopped dead in her tracks and every ounce of color drained from her face until her face was somewhere between pasty and ashen. "Genna? What is it?"

She stared at the man standing not twenty feet in front of them looking at neckties, feeling her insides freeze-dry and shatter into a million pieces. Allan.

"Genna?"

Jared's anxious voice jolted her. "Nothing. It's nothing," she managed, trying to turn him down the underwear aisle. "Can we go this way?"

But Jared didn't budge, and Allan Corrigan turned and looked right at her.

Suddenly there was a beefy arm drawing her against a beefier body, and Jared pressed a kiss to her forehead and said for her ears only, "Introduce me, Gen."

Bewildered, she looked up at him to find azure eyes filled with gentle understanding, and a satin-soft smile. He kissed the tip of her nose. She knew that to anyone watching they appeared like a pair of lovers totally absorbed in each other.

He nudged her forward, saying through his teeth, "Look happy, darling."

She plastered on an enormous smile as they approached the last man on earth she ever wanted to see. "Why, Allan! Is that you?" she said brightly, gagging on the words.

"Genna." He straightened, still holding a maroon paisley tie. He wasn't as tall as Jared, and his pinstripe suit emphasized his slender build. Everything about Allan was neat and businesslike, from his carefully combed but thinning blond hair, right down to his Lloyd and Haig shoes. He was undeniably handsome in a pale, thin sort of way. "How are you?"

I want to vomit. "Fine. Wonderful." She smiled wider, wondering if her face would break. Then she'd feel really stupid, standing in the middle of a big department store with no face.

Jared pinched her, a phony smile in place and murder in his eyes. "Introduce me to your . . . friend, honey."

"What? Oh! Yes! Jared, this is Allan Corrigan, an old . . . person . . . I used to know," she said lamely. "Allan, this is Jared Hennessy."

"The quarterback?" Allan blurted out in obvious surprise.

Jared gave him an unpleasant, unamused twitch of the lips. "That's right," he drawled, the words clearly translating into *of course, you stupid jerk.*

Genna wanted to laugh hysterically. Allan was always so smug. Nothing ever impressed him. And he *never* blurted. Now he appeared to shrink in embarrassment.

Jared, on the other hand, appeared positively intimidating. He had the look of a possessive male whose territory was being threatened. His narrowed gaze pinned Allan with an icy stare. "Just how well do you know my Genna?"

The subtle emphasis on "my" was perfect, Genna thought, giving rein to a mischievous streak. Allan took an involuntary step back. She patted Jared's stomach reassuringly. "Now, J.J., don't go getting nasty. This is a public place."

Allan's Adam's apple bobbed nervously in his throat. His hand crushed the silk tie he'd been considering buying. "Oh—really—Mr. Hennessy, there's no reason—I mean, Genna and I—there's nothing—"

Jared's nostrils flared, his chest puffed up. "She was *nothing* to you?"

He charged two steps before Genna dropped her bags, got him by the waistband of his jeans, and threw her weight back, swinging them both around in a circle. Allan had the paisley necktie by both ends, holding it horizontally in front of him as if the thin silk would provide him some sort of protection.

"That's not what I meant!" he squealed.

"Honestly, Jared," Genna scolded, letting go of him. She stooped to pick up her bags. "I'm going to have to put you on a leash if you're going to act this way."

Barely taking his eyes off Allan, Jared leaned down and pressed a quick kiss on her lips. "Come on, honey," he said with a growl. "Let's go home."

Genna shot a glance at Allan and choked back a giggle. He looked like a man who had just narrowly escaped a close encounter with a grizzly bear. His hair was practically standing on end. "Nice to see you, Allan," she said as Jared's arm went possessively around her waist and he started to herd her away.

"See you around, Corrigan." J.J. bared his teeth in a parody of a smile. "By the way, that's a bad-looking tie. You ought to buy it, it goes with your suit."

On their way across the windy parking lot, Genna, on the verge of nervous hysteria, began to giggle. The giggles built into uncontrollable laughter, and she had to stop and lean against Jared's car, holding her stomach. Jared dug into his pocket and produced a mangled package of M&M's. He munched on the candy while he watched Genna be hysterical.

"Oh—oh!" she gasped for breath. "Poor Allan! He looked like he'd just come out of electroshock therapy! He thought you were going to tear him apart right there in public! What a wonderful act!"

Jared managed to twitch up the corners of his mouth. He wondered what Genna would do if she knew how little of it had been an act. He'd never been jealous or possessive in his life, but, Lord, he'd *wanted* to take Corrigan apart just for knowing Genna. It seemed she brought out the primitive in him. She'd probably set a new women's track record by running away from him if she found that out.

The air coming into and out of her lungs was more regular now, and Genna straightened and wiped the tears from her face with the back of her hand. With the initial giddiness out of her system she was able to think about what had happened. Jared had pushed her into a situation she'd been dreading for nearly a year, and he'd brought her out of it without a scratch.

"Why did you do that for me?" she asked with wonder.

Jared reached around her and unlocked the door of the Mercedes, then stood back and gave her a long, considering look. He reached out and tenderly brushed a lock of wavy hair from her face. "We're a team, Genna. Team players stick up for each other."

Genna knew that had she been alone, she would have ducked down that underwear aisle to avoid Allan, and she would have spent the next month and a half branding herself a coward. Jared had not only spared her that, but he had also won back a little of the self-esteem she had lost when Allan had ended their relationship. Allan had left her feeling inadequate as a woman. Jared had erased that feeling.

I do . . . L . . . love him, she thought. She raised a hand and tenderly brushed the back of her fingers down the lean plane of his cheek. Magic skittered down her arm. Awareness of him trembled through her. She wondered idly in the back of her mind what the school board would have to say if she were arrested for attacking the man in a parking lot.

Jared broke the sudden sexual tension, his wicked grin slashing across his face. "Let's go for ice cream, Teach."

Genna didn't say five words all the way home to Jared's. He didn't try to break the silence, leaving her to her thoughts, but he studied her as he drove toward Tory Hills. What had this Corrigan guy been to her? A lover? More? What had the bastard done to her to make her bolt at the sight of him?

She just sat there staring out the window, one foot out of its loafer rubbing absently against her sore ankle. Damn it, she shouldn't have given up her crutches so soon, he thought. He'd said as much, but there was no telling her anything; she had a stubborn streak a mile wide. Of course he loved her for it.

Loved her. The thought hit him with all the finesse of a linebacker. No wonder he'd wanted to dismember Genna's old flame. He was in love with her—as in head over heels. He'd set out to win her interest because she was a challenge to him. Now he realized he had to win her love or he'd lose his heart.

I *will* do it, he told himself with fierce determination.

If she wasn't still in love with that puny jerk, Corrigan.

That thought scared him more than a little bit. Corrigan was some kind of dull business type. The guy's ties were more interesting than his personality. He was exactly what Genna was looking for.

Jared steered the Mercedes into his garage and parked it beside his black Corvette. He turned the motor off and asked a little nervously, "Want to come in for a drink or something?"

Only if it's stronger than root beer, she thought, "Sure."

She followed Jared into the house, limping a little, but the pain in her ankle was nothing compared to the remembered pain of her affair with Allan. She stood looking out the living room window, not seeing anything, thinking back on how wrong she had been about him.

She wasn't the sort of person who went into relationships without a lot of thought. She had been so sure she and Allan had wanted the same things out of their relationship. How could she have been so wrong? Was she really that lacking in judgment?

Jared went around the room turning on lamps. It wasn't late yet, but the wind had blown in a thick layer of dark clouds, and the summer air smelled of approaching rain.

He turned for the kitchen, intending to go pour their drinks, but he stopped himself. He couldn't stand the silence any longer. Maybe he could tease her out of it. Maybe that way he could weasel some answers out of her without putting his heart on the chopping block. If she were still in love with that suit rack, he wanted to know about it now.

"So, this Corrigan guy," he said lightly, cursing inwardly at the way her shoulders tensed. He forced a chuckle. "*That's* what you're looking for? *That's* what you want in a man? I'm being cast aside in favor of a balding CPA? That hurts, Genna. That really hurts."

Not really wanting to say anything at all, Genna fell back on her same old worn-out argument, though there was no conviction in her voice. "There's nothing wrong in wanting a stable professional man."

"So marry a jockey," he quipped, wincing at the lame joke.

Genna didn't even try to think of a snappy comeback. She was too busy trying not to burst into tears. She had honestly believed that Allan Corrigan was the man of her dreams, yet he had hurt her unbelievably. How many other things had she been wrong about?

"Gen?" Jared's voice was soft and gentle, questioning and apologetic. His breath stirred the hair behind her ear. She felt his hands settle on her shoulders and had to fight to keep from leaning back into his strength.

"No," she said hoarsely. "Allan Corrigan isn't at all what I'm looking for. I thought he was once. I made a big mistake."

"Make that two," he murmured, turning her to face him. He tilted her chin up and gently brushed a stray tear from her cheek with the pad of his thumb. "You can't judge a book by its cover, Teach. You never know what might be lurking under the dust jacket."

He was so right, she thought as she looked up at him with the tremulous beginnings of a smile. She'd have sworn Allan was as true-blue as the suits he wore, but he'd turned out to be as shallow as a puddle after a summer shower. On the other hand, no one could have convinced her a man of sterling character resided inside the uncommon exterior of Jared Hennessy, until she'd seen it for herself. She had been wrong about him and she was glad.

She welcomed Jared's kiss. Something about it was like coming home. With his strong arms holding her, she felt safe and protected, dainty and womanly. With his lips claiming hers, she forgot she'd ever been kissed by another man.

As she returned that kiss, her arms winding around his neck, Genna felt the wall of stubborn resistance inside her crumble and dissolve. She gave in to what she'd known for a long time now: It didn't matter that Jared wore a diamond earring instead of a diamond tie tack. He was caring and considerate. He was intelligent and talented. Incorrigible, but not irresponsible. He was worth a dozen Allan Corrigans.

Acceptance lifted a two-ton burden from her heart. She smiled against his lips. "Mmmm . . . you taste good."

He nibbled along her jawline, pulling her even closer, every soft curve of her fitting perfectly against him. Sighing at the sweet torture, he buried a hand in the luxurious waves of her chestnut hair. His lips teased the delicate shell of her ear. "I want to make love with you, Genna . . . what do you want?"

His breath held fast and hard in his throat as he waited and hoped and prayed.

Genna pressed her cheek to his chest and listened to the thunder of his heart. She smiled and looked up at him, her own heart skipping at the vulnerability in his beautiful blue eyes.

"I want you to make love with me, Jared."

He grinned. She grinned.

"Okay," he said resignedly, giving a comic shrug of his broad shoulders. "You talked me into it."

Each with an arm around the other's waist, Jared led the way to his room, the one room in the house Genna had shied away from. It was much neater than she had imagined. There was a shirt over the back of a chair, and a pair of beat-to-death running shoes had been abandoned on the dark gray carpet, but no clothes overflowed the drawers of the oak dresser and the bed was made.

The bed. Genna smiled. It was an enormous oak-framed water bed mounted on a high pedestal base. She arched a brow at Jared.

"For my bad back," he insisted.

He switched on the small brass lamps on the bedside tables, casting a soft golden light around the room. Then they stood facing each other, holding hands, smiling and inching closer and closer together.

There was no hurry, no nervousness, only the pleasant tingle of mutual anticipation. It was as if they had been lovers for years. Sweet kisses were traded and trailed over mouth, cheek, and throat, as fingers fumbled with buttons.

As glad as Genna had been to see Jared wearing a normal, light blue oxford-cloth shirt, she was even happier when it was off him so at last her hands could touch his magnificent chest. It was a masculine masterpiece, bronzed and beautiful, and lightly sprigged with black hair. She watched hungrily as her fingertips traced the definite lines and ridges of muscle. He was tan and hard and all man, his skin smooth and warm. She thought that if she lived to be one hundred, she'd never get enough of touching him.

Jared held still for her explorations, watching her smoky eyes darken with desire. This was what he'd been waiting for, for Genna to want to take the next step in their relationship. Now he could scarcely believe it was happening. Her palm pressed against the springy chest hair. One fingertip traveled to circle and tease a dark nipple. His breath caught as her thumb brushed the pebble-hard bud of flesh. Her head dipped, and her warm, wet tongue darted out to caress it. Still he held on to his control until she looked up him, her eyes impossibly huge and dark.

Growling low in his throat, he bent and kissed her, his hands ridding her of her white cotton blouse and lacy bra. Their sighs mingled in the still room as flesh met flesh, soft breasts pressed against unyielding muscle, satisfying one need. For a moment they simply held each other, savoring this first plateau, hands stroking backs as they nuzzled and breathed in the clean warm scents of man and woman.

Genna tipped her head back and begged another kiss, this one deeper than the last. She offered him access to the sweetness of her mouth and trembled with delight when he accepted, his lips caressing hers, his tongue sliding deep inside. She arched against Jared like a cat begging to be stroked. Her breasts ached for his touch. He complied readily, his hands cupping the tender flesh, kneading, rubbing the swollen red tips against his chest.

She moaned her pleasure and her need, pressing against him. Waves of anticipation radiated from her belly, where Jared's arousal nudged at her through his jeans. Somewhere far, far back in her mind Genna realized she had never felt quite this way. She had never felt quite so bold in her sexuality. Jared was so overwhelmingly male, he drew out all that was female in her.

"Unzip me, honey," he instructed her against her ear.

Genna let her desire consume her, let it take control. She felt no need to hold back or be shy with him. Eagerly her hands went to his waistband to do his bidding, working the button free and peeling the zipper down. She didn't hesitate to push his jeans and briefs out of their way.

Somehow Jared managed the same task, stripping Genna's khaki chinos and her panties down over her hips. They came together again, each aching to touch the other. He nearly crushed her in his embrace as they reached another plateau and the passion began to boil higher. Genna raised on tiptoe and moved against him, loving the feel of his smooth, hard maleness pressed between them, as Jared's tongue slowly plunged in and out of her mouth in the rhythm of love.

Breaking apart, they each stepped out of their pants. Jared yanked back the navy coverlet and dark gray sheets, and helped Genna onto the bed. It rippled gently beneath them as they settled down. Jared stretched out beside her, one leg thrown over hers. He planted kisses along her collarbone. His hand stroked her waist, her flank, slipped between her parted thighs, his fingers brushing through the tangle of dark curls there.

Genna gasped at the pleasure. Jared caressed her intimately. His thumb found her most sensitive flesh and rubbed the aching bud as he eased a finger up inside her, testing her readiness and heightening it at once.

"This will be so special, sweetheart," he whispered against her throat.

"Yes," she said between breaths, her hands clutching at his back. Special and so right. Already she knew a completeness deep in her soul that she had never felt before. Jared was special. He was her friend and he would be her lover.

Moaning, she turned to him, her hand seeking and finding his arousal. She wanted to give him pleasure, wanted him to know the consuming desire that pleasure created. Jared groaned and let his teeth graze her shoulder as her hand stroked and gently tugged at him.

He wanted her. His blood was on fire, but he felt no desire to rush. He wanted to touch and taste and please every inch of her. Time was of no importance. She was finally going to be his. He planned to savor the moments.

Genna felt the same. It seemed her whole body ached for him, but she wanted no quick burst of satisfaction. These feelings building inside her were too intense, too wonderful to use up greedily.

With a shift of his hips, Jared was kneeling between her thighs. He kissed her, then dragged his kiss to her ear, where he nibbled and nuzzled.

"Are you protected, honey?"

Genna murmured a distracted yes, then pulled his mouth back to hers to drink in the warm, fresh taste of him. He pulled away, sliding down her body, seeking out one breast then the other. His hands molded around the full, ripe mounds as he kissed them and breathed in their powder-soft scent. With maddening slowness he drew his tongue around the dark areola, finally closing his lips over her throbbing nipple.

She cried out as he sucked her, and held his head to her when he was going to pull away. Her eyes squeezed shut as the exquisite sensations shot through her like jolts of electricity, burning a path straight to the pit of her stomach.

Jared slid down, planting lingering kisses across the feminine swell of tummy below her navel, then lower. She opened herself to him, offering the sweet treasure of her womanhood to his seeking mouth, gasping his name and arching up for him.

Then his mouth was on hers as he eased into the silken heat of her an inch at a time until she was full of him. His hands slipped beneath her, angling her hips. He sank deeper still.

"Jared!" She gasped softly.

"Am I hurting you, sweetheart?"

"No," she whispered, reaching up to touch his cheek with a trembling hand. "So perfect."

His eyes held hers. Sweat beaded on his brow. "Perfect, my sweet, sweet Genna."

Her heart overflowing with love for him, Genna could only murmur his name as their bodies began to move together toward fulfillment. They moved in beautiful harmony as the pleasure built, carrying them higher and higher until they strained together for the peak, and then soared beyond it.

It was perfect.

Afterward they lay together in a tangle of legs and sheets, Genna's head pressed to the hollow of Jared's shoulder as he stroked her back. Contentment overrode the need for conversation. For a long while they did nothing more than bask in the sweet afterglow of their loving.

Jared was the one who broke the silence. Genna had given herself to him physically, but there were still emotional barriers between them. He was determined to take them down even if it meant hearing about a past love. "Tell me about what happened between you and Corrigan."

Startled, Genna lifted her head, her eyes searching, her heart beating at a frantic pace. Did she dare tell Jared?

Sensing her uncertainty, Jared gently stroked her cheek and said, "It's okay, honey, you can tell me. We're friends, remember?"

Yes, Genna thought, easing her head back to his shoulder, she could tell Jared. He was her friend first.

"It was just a case of me thinking things were more serious between us than they really were," she said softly. It sounded so simple but it had been so difficult. The deep bruise to her heart and her pride had never quite healed. The experience had left a dark blotch on her sense of self-esteem and on her belief in her own judgment, all because she had made the mistake of assuming "I love you" applied out of the bedroom as well as in it. She had sworn to never make that mistake again. "That problem wouldn't have been so hard to straighten out, except . . ."

Jared kissed her forehead and wrapped his arms around her, waiting for her to continue. "Except what?" he coaxed her gently, not in the least prepared for her answer.

"I got pregnant," she whispered, tears filling her eyes at the way Jared tensed beneath her. Was he thinking what Allan had thought? She hoped with all her heart he wasn't, feared with all her heart he was. Her voice trembled with both emotions as she went on. "It was an accident, a fluke. I didn't plan it, I swear."

His arms tightened around her automatically as he struggled to swallow a major dose of guilt. It was obvious Genna believed he would think the worst and that Corrigan *had.* Jared wanted to damn the bastard to hell, but how could he? Hadn't he always harbored the belief that Elaine had gotten pregnant on purpose?

"I didn't," Genna murmured. "I wouldn't do that. It wouldn't be fair to anyone, especially the baby."

"I know you wouldn't, Gen," he assured her, hurting for her.

She gave a humorless laugh. "Allan didn't. He came right out and accused me of trying to trap him into marrying me. He was furious. He said a lot of ugly things, culminating with 'You got yourself into this, you can get yourself out of it.' And then he left."

Jared wasn't having any trouble cursing Corrigan now. If he ever saw the lowlife jerk again, he'd be hard pressed not to snap his neck like a chicken bone. Genna would have been frightened and upset, and that damned three-piece suit had left her in the lurch!

He tried to keep his rising temper under control as he asked, "What'd you do?"

A sad smile curved her mouth against his chest. She had wanted the child even if Allan hadn't. And she had been prepared to make sacrifices to keep her baby. But ultimately the decision had not been hers to make. "Nothing," she said. "Life is full of little ironies, you know. Two days after I told Allan the good news, I miscarried. Thank heaven Amy and I were in Hartford at the time. No one in Tory Hills ever knew, or I would have been out of a job on top of everything else."

"They'd have fired you?" he asked in surprise.

She tilted her head up so she could look at him. "Do you know any unmarried, pregnant kindergarten teachers?"

He thought about it for a minute before answering. The sexual revolution notwithstanding, Tory Hills was a conservative small town. The good folk here would have taken a dim view of the situation. "I see your point," he said.

"So anyway," she said with forced brightness as she propped herself up on an elbow and looked down at him with vulnerable blue eyes, "that's the tale of my sordid past. Have I ruined the evening?"

Jared stared up at her, aching for her, for the pain she'd suffered. She'd been through a hell of a lot and had come out on top. He'd been right from the start. She had *it.* Genna Hastings was one very special lady. And now she was his.

"No," he whispered, pulling her down so he could kiss her. As she stretched out on top of him, he felt passion begin anew, even sweeter than before. His hand stroked down her back then up, his fingers tangling in the thick silk of her hair. "I'm your friend, honey. I want you to know you can tell me anything. I won't ever stop being your friend." He wanted to tell her he loved her, but he held back, afraid she might not want to hear that just yet.

"I know," she whispered, stringing kisses slowly up his chest to his mouth. "Thank you."

"Thank you," he said, "for sharing part of yourself with me."

And they both knew he wasn't talking about the act of love that joined their bodies once more, but the trust she'd given him in telling her story.

Seven

It was eleven forty-five when the phone beside Jared's bed rang and jolted them both awake. He reached for it and groaned a sleepy, " 'Lo?"

"Jared, it's Amy. Sorry if I woke you, but—"

"Is Alyssa all right?" he demanded, coming fully awake and sitting upright in bed. Genna sat up, too, pulling the gray sheet around her.

"No. She's pretty upset—"

"I'll be right there." He was out of bed and pulling his jeans on before the receiver hit the cradle.

"Jared, what is it?" Genna asked, fear making her shiver in spite of the bedcovers. Jared's features were grim as he yanked on his clothes.

"Alyssa's had another nightmare," he said, shoving his feet into his running shoes. He didn't even look at her as he bolted from the room.

For a moment Genna sat back against the pillows. So this was why he had been reluctant to let Alyssa spend the night away from home. *Another* nightmare. No doubt it was related to the accident she'd been in that had killed her mother. Poor little lamb, Genna thought, aching to comfort the little girl. That was Jared's department, though. Well, she would do what she could, she decided, slipping out of bed to dress.

Across the street Jared didn't bother to knock on the Dennisons' front door. He practically stormed the place, bursting in and striding into the living room to the couch where Amy sat trying to calm Alyssa. His daughter was sobbing as if her entire world had come to an end.

"Come here, baby," Jared crooned, scooping her into his arms and holding her tight as she cried on his shoulder. "Daddy's here, sweetheart."

"I think she had a nightmare," Amy said, handing Jared Alyssa's little suitcase.

"I know," he nodded, giving her an apologetic look. "I'm sorry, Amy."

Amy shook her head, almost in tears herself at Alyssa's heartwrenching sobs. She reached up and brushed the little girl's hair back from her tear-drenched face. "It's okay, honey. You can come back another time."

Her words only made Jared's daughter cry all the harder.

"I'm—not—a—big—girl," she said between hiccups as they crossed the street.

"Sure you are, honey," Jared whispered, his heart breaking as he held Alyssa in his arms, sobs racking her little body.

"Nooooo!" she wailed.

Genna met them at the door and followed them to Alyssa's room, where she had turned the carousel horse lamp on and the frilly covers of the canopied bed back. She leaned against the doorframe, wanting to be near enough to help but not wanting to intrude.

Jared toed off his sneakers and sat on the bed, leaning back against the carved white headboard and stretching his legs out, Alyssa still clinging to his shoulder. He tried to comfort and quiet her with soft words and kisses as his hand stroked over the cloud of her midnight hair. He looked up once, his gaze, full of pain and helplessness, meeting Genna's, so longing to help. Then he squeezed his eyes shut to keep his own tears at bay. He could handle two-hundred-plus-pound football players running over him with the zeal of a freight train, but it tore him apart to hear his little girl cry.

"It was—the—bad dream—Daddy," Alyssa said, sliding down onto his lap and pressing her wet face to his chest, her tears staining his shirt.

"I know it was, muffin," he murmured. "It's all gone now."

One small hand smoothed over the white eyelet nightgown that had been purchased for her big night, as the tears in Alyssa's blue eyes welled up and spilled over again. "I'm not a big girl."

"Sure you are, Lyss," Jared said thickly. "Even grown-ups have bad dreams sometimes."

He dried her tears with a handkerchief from his hip pocket. She was nearly all cried out. He had unfortunately gone through this enough to know. Pulling the covers up around them, he tucked Alyssa's worn-out rag doll in her arms.

"Here's Dollie," he whispered tenderly, kissing his daughter's hair and hugging her close. She still cried in fits and spurts. "Should we play The Game, muffin?"

She nodded.

"Okay. Let's close our eyes—"

"Nooo!" she sobbed, so clearly frightened that Genna had to wonder what terrible visions came to Alyssa when she closed her eyes.

"We have to," Jared persisted gently. "Remember? We close our eyes and what do we see?"

The crescent of long inky lashes glistening with tears fluttered down against Alyssa's cheek. "Th—the sky."

"That's right. A beautiful blue sky," He spoke in a slow, soothing cadence, his warm, smoky voice coaxing his little girl to relax, lulling her to sleep. His hand stroked her hair over and over. "With big, fluffy white clouds.

"What else do we see?"

"Grass . . . and flowers."

"Lots of flowers. All different kinds and colors; blue and yellow and pink . . . It's a meadow. And it's warm and nice, and the grass is blowing over in the wind. What else do we see? What's in the grass?"

"Bunnies," Alyssa said, the thumb of one hand inching toward her mouth. ". . . And they're hopping and playing."

"Are they having fun?"

She nodded against his chest. "And puppies too."

"Rolling in the grass like Flurry does?"

The thumb found its target on the second nod and she was asleep.

Jared held her for a moment longer, finally kissing the top of her head and easing himself out from under her. He left the lamp on low and went to Genna, looking like he'd run a marathon, his wide shoulders sagging, his face pale and drawn.

She put her arms around him and held him close, feeling ten times stronger than he and knowing she had to be that strong for him now because he just didn't have it left in him. He lowered his head to her shoulder.

"Hell of a way to end the evening. I'm sorry."

"Don't worry about me," she said, patting his broad back. "Does this happen often?"

He broke the embrace and leaned back against the doorjamb, shoving his hands into his pockets. "Not as often as it did at first. It used to be every night."

"Is it about the accident?"

He nodded, looking down at his bare feet on the powder-blue rug. "They were broadsided on the driver's side. There was a lot of blood. . . ." He swore softly. "I'd give anything for Alyssa not to have been in that car. I'd give anything to make the nightmares go away."

He turned his head to watch his daughter sleep. Genna thought he looked almost as vulnerable as Alyssa. *This is the same man who was so strong and sure making love with you not two hours ago,* she reminded herself. Her heart ached with love for him. She thought back to what he'd said about them being a team and team players sticking up for each other. She wanted to offer him support now, as he had done for her.

"You handled it really well," she said, meaning it.

"I do my best," he said with a sigh, wishing his best were good enough. Would Simone Harcourt's best be better? Or would she leave Alyssa alone at night to face the "bad dream" herself?

• • •

The trouble had been brewing for three days. Genna had seen it coming, had sensed the tension in the air, but had thought of no way to defuse the bomb.

Beginning the morning after the nightmare, Jared's darling daughter had turned into a tiny tyrant—but only with Jared. She cheerfully obeyed Bernice and Genna, but defied her father at every turn. If he wanted a meal, she wasn't hungry. If he said it was day, she said it was night. She unfailingly did the exact opposite of what Jared asked of her. Where he was concerned, Alyssa was the most contrary creature on earth.

At first Jared let it slide. It was simply a bad mood on Alyssa's part. As the days passed and the mood seemed only to worsen, he began losing his patience. Genna watched helplessly as he became more confused and hurt and frustrated by his daughter's behavior. She had a pretty good idea what the root of the problem was, but Jared didn't want to hear advice on the subject. He was so determined to be a good father, he viewed the need for advice as a weakness on his part. So Genna forced herself to stand on the sidelines and wait for the battle.

Meanwhile, they worked on Jared's house. Pictures were hung, a dining room table and chairs purchased. A new set of china filled the shelves of the cupboard, along with crystal. Jared's football trophies and photos were put in an oak and glass cabinet near his desk in the spacious living room.

Genna tried to involve Jared as much as she could in making selections for the house. After all, it was his home. Even though he had asked her to do the job, she found herself feeling guilty about making the changes necessary to give Jared and his house a normal look. Jared's bizarre outfits and decorating ideas were part of who he was. Did anyone else really have the right to tell him to act otherwise? Still, it was his money, and he seemed sincere about changing his lifestyle.

"The mannequin has got to go," Genna said for the third time. She and Jared stood on the front porch arguing about lawn beauty. Having convinced him to get rid of most of the flamingos, she had held off on the issue of Candy, but Candy's day had come.

"Aw, come on, Gen! Candy and I have been together since college!"

Genna just looked at him, crossing her arms over her chest and impatiently tapping her sneakered foot. Jared tried staring her down, but she was, after all, a teacher—one of the world's greatest stare-down artists. He glanced away, then back at her, a stirring of desire reminding him it had been too long since their first night together. She was so darn cute when she had that stubborn little tilt to her chin. She wore a pair of jeans that were almost white with age and carefully patched. They molded to her body as if they were in love with her. And she wore the same old navy polo shirt she'd had on the night they'd made out on her kitchen floor.

He looked from Genna to Candy, who sat on her lawn chair with her hands in her lap, her head tilted as if she were listening to them argue her fate. Dammit, he liked the mannequin. This "being normal" business was getting on his nerves. If he wanted a mannequin on his front porch, why shouldn't he be able to have one? She wasn't hurting anybody.

"Maybe she could wear something more sedate," he suggested. He regarded Candy with a critical eye. "Picture her in a soft, flowered dress. Something very feminine. And a big straw hat maybe."

"She would still be a mannequin."

"But a very nicely dressed one."

"Normal people don't keep mannequins on their porches."

Jared scowled, looking at the houses down the block. "Theron Ralston has a *yard jockey*," he accused derisively.

"Theron Ralston is a bigot," Genna said. "He is also on the school board, and I can tell you right now what he'll say about a man who wears an earring and keeps a mannequin on his porch. He'll say you're a homosexual Communist on drugs."

"Well, it's none of his damn business anyway," Jared

groused, patting Candy fondly on top of her blonde wig.

"No, it's not," Genna agreed. "But you hired me to do a job and I'm doing it. Impossible as it may seem at times, you are going to have the outward appearance of being a normal person when I'm through." She frowned at the black T-shirt that clung to his muscular torso. A hog rode a Harley-Davidson above the words BORN TO BE WILD. "Candy goes," she said firmly. "I don't care where, as long as she's out of my sight."

Jared's eyes suddenly glittered with devilment and he slid an arm around Genna's waist, his smile wreaking havoc with her pulse. "Tell the truth, Teach. You're jealous."

"Of a mannequin?" She gave him a look. "That's sick, Hennessy."

"Don't worry, honey," he went on. "It's purely platonic between Candy and me."

"I certainly hope so," she said dryly, "or you're going to need more than my help to become normal."

Chuckling like a maniac, Jared pinched her bottom and danced away from her halfhearted swing at him. He hopped off the porch onto the sidewalk. "If I get Candy off the porch, can I have another flamingo?"

"Absolutely not. Who do I look like, Monte Hall?"

A lump of black dirt landed on Jared's Nikes. His teasing smile vanished as his eyes landed on Alyssa, who sat digging up the soil around a shrub with a shovel from her sandbox.

"Alyssa, what are you doing?"

Genna bit her lip at the hard edge of impatience in Jared's voice. His frayed temper was dangerously close to snapping. The mutinous look on Alyssa's face gave Genna the sick feeling that the showdown was about to take place.

"Digging," Alyssa snapped, not looking up from her task.

"You can't dig in the yard." Jared reined in his anger and tried more gently. "Why don't you go dig in your sandbox?"

"I hate it!"

She might as well have slapped him, Genna thought. Jared had spent a whole day lovingly slaving over building that sandbox, and Alyssa knew it. She was deliberately lashing out at him, and emotionally, it didn't matter that she was only five and he was thirty, her words still hurt him.

Jared went pale. A muscle worked furiously in his jaw. It took every ounce of willpower Genna had to keep from intervening. She loved them both and hated to see either suffer, but she knew this had to come to a head.

"Alyssa, go to the backyard," he said in a tight voice.

"No."

"Alyssa, go to—"

Splat. More black dirt crumbled over his shoes.

"Alyssa Hennessy," Jared said menacingly, yanking his daughter to her feet. "Go to your room."

Alyssa wriggled out of his grasp. She threw her shovel at him and yelled, *"No!"*

"Do it, Alyssa!" He took one threatening step in her direction, and Alyssa burst into tears and made a beeline for Genna's house.

Jared wheeled around and watched her go, his chest heaving, his face red. Methodically, he bent and scooped up the dirt at his feet, his hands squeezing it into a hard ball. Genna flinched as he swore viciously, then turned and flung the ball of dirt down the street, narrowly missing the Ralstons' yard jockey and sending Mrs. Ralston's poodle, Clyde, shrieking for the shelter of their porch. Jared didn't even spare Genna a glance as he yanked open the screen door and stormed into his house.

Seconds later Bernice came out looking as if she'd seen a ghost. She leaned back against the screen, her generous bosom working like a bellows, her arms spread wide at her sides as if to keep a monster from coming out the door.

"You okay, Bernice?" Genna asked.

"Oh—oh—sure, honey," she puffed. "I'm not taking any chances is all. I think maybe I'll go bowling or something."

"Good idea."

"Better than staying here and getting my head handed to me." She eased away from the door, casting a nervous glance over her shoulder. "Maybe you can get the boss to go out for dinner. Or just toss him some raw meat through the door."

"Don't worry about it, Bernice. I'll take care of him. He just needs some time alone."

Genna slipped quietly into her kitchen and went in search of the source of all the commotion. Alyssa was kneeling on the carpet with her face on Genna's love seat, crying her heart out. Without a word Genna sat down and reached her arms out to Jared's daughter. They were filled immediately.

"I want my mommy!" Alyssa sobbed over and over.

"I know you do, honey," Genna said, idly stroking the girl's black tresses. "I know you miss her, baby."

"I want her to come back from heaven. Make her come back!"

Genna's heart twisted. This wasn't the kind of lesson a little one should have to learn. "I'm sorry, it doesn't work like that, Lyss. I wish it did. Are you angry with her for going to heaven?"

The little head bobbed against Genna's breast as the sobs came harder.

"I understand that, honey. You don't have to feel bad. But you know your mommy wouldn't have left you if she'd had a choice. I'm sure she loved you very much."

"I miss her."

"I know."

For a long while they sat silently, Genna giving Alyssa time to cope with the feelings that had been building inside her like a head of steam.

"I love my daddy," Alyssa whispered, sniffling.

Genna handed her a tissue and hugged her close. "He knows that, baby. He loves you too. But you know you hurt his feelings, don't you?"

Alyssa nodded, the tears coming again. "I'm naughty. He's angry and he won't want me to be his little girl anymore."

"No, honey, that's not true," Genna assured her.

"You'll have to tell him you're sorry, but he'll forgive you. And I know for sure he'll always want you to be his little girl."

Eventually Alyssa ran out of tears and misgivings, and fell asleep in Genna's arms. Genna laid her on the love seat, ignoring the child's dirty knees and sneakers, and covered her bare legs with a quilt.

The afternoon sky had grown dark with the prospect of a shower, and the living room was cloaked in cool shadows, but Genna didn't turn on any lamps. As the rain began, she went to the kitchen to work off some of her own frustrations by baking a cake. When that task was finished she sat down on the couch across from Alyssa, curling her legs under her like a cat, and waited.

It wasn't long before Jared walked in the back door. His hair was damp. Raindrops had made dark spots on his T-shirt and jeans. The cold gray light that seeped in through the windows fell on the drawn lines of his face. He looked as if he'd just lost his last and best friend. The mischief that usually filled his blue eyes had been replaced with an unbelievable anguish. He said nothing, didn't seem to notice Genna curled up on the couch.

She watched him as he stood gazing down at his daughter. He looked as if a terrible war raged inside him and he was terrified of the outcome. He reached out once toward the sleeping child, but his hand fell back to his side like a marionette's whose string had been cut.

After a moment he turned and wandered around the living room, stopping in front of a curio cabinet that sat against the far wall below the stairs. He stood staring at the cabinet with its collection of porcelain animals, his eyes traveling across each shelf, taking in horses, sheep, dogs, rabbits. Genna went to sit on the third step so he would know she was there for him when he was ready to talk.

"I don't know," he said at last, his voice huskier than usual. "I—I'm trying *so* hard to be a good father to her."

"You are a good father to her."

"Oh, yeah?" he asked with a caustic laugh, still not looking at Genna. "Then how come I feel like a louse? How come I never know the right thing to say or do, and I always seem to blow it when it counts?"

Maybe everything had always come too easily for him, Jared thought. He'd never known what it was to struggle for something he really wanted. His profession came naturally to him; all the moves came instinctively. Now he wanted more than anything to be a good father and he had no idea how to go about it. He didn't have a clue about what he was doing wrong. It was as if he suddenly couldn't read a defense, his line was crumbling around him, and he was left holding the ball and not knowing what to do with it.

Maybe he just wasn't cut out to be a father.

Maybe he didn't have *it*.

Maybe Alyssa would be better off with her aunt.

He flinched as a hand settled on his arm. Genna's hand.

"You're a very good father to Alyssa, Jared," she said, gently leading him back to the couch, where they both sat down. "You're just not much of a mother."

Now his brain was starting to dysfunction. He stared at Genna, bemused.

"Listen," Genna said, tucking her bare feet under her Indian-style. "Alyssa just lost her mother. She's afraid, hurt, angry. That's a big load for a five-year-old to handle. On top of that, she's gone from being cared for by a woman to being cared for by a man. There's a big difference, in case you hadn't noticed.

"You're doing a good job. Maybe you're a little too lenient—"

He scowled immediately at the insinuation, but his look softened just as quickly. "Do you think I spoil her?"

"Just a little." Genna smiled gently.

"I guess I do. It's just that I've hardly had any time with her and I like buying her presents and stuff." He took a sudden interest in his fingernails as he added, "And I want her to like me."

Genna looked from father to sleeping daughter and

back. "Lyssa loves you, Jared. She just needs a little time to adjust. You both do."

The sense of what she was saying managed to sink into Jared's befuddled brain. He gave her a feeble smile. "How'd you get to be so damn smart?"

"Psych minor," she nodded, letting her own smile coax his to blossom.

He grinned. "Is that gonna cost me extra, Teach?"

"I'll put it on your bill."

The grin melted away and his look was one of pure need as he reached out to her. "Put this on the bill too, will you? I need a hug." He pulled her into his arms, pressing his head to her shoulder as she kneeled unsteadily on the couch.

"I got another letter from Simone's lawyer today," he said, holding her tighter. "They're going ahead with the suit. They think they can prove I'm not fit to keep Lyssa."

"Oh, Jared," she said with a sigh, cursing the unseen woman whose timing couldn't have been worse.

"What if I'm not?" came his tortured whisper.

"You listen to me, Jared Jay Hennessy," Genna said in her sternest teacher voice, pushing him back so she could glare at him. "You may be a little offbeat—okay, a *lot* offbeat—but I can't name one man who'd make a better father to that little girl. Now get that through your thick head."

"Yes, ma'am," he said, smiling, though his eyes glistened with tears, as did Genna's. He laughed. "Geez, I think we're gonna cry."

They both laughed at that, stray tears spilling over their boundaries. Then Jared pulled Genna to him in a crushing embrace, burying his face in her hair. "Oh, Gen, I'm so scared of losing her."

"You won't lose her," she whispered, praying she was right.

With a supreme effort Jared blinked away the tears that had threatened, then sniffed, raising his head. He sat back, his face taking on the keen look of a hound on a scent, and murmured three words, "Apple spice cake."

"With apple frosting."
"Oh, wow."
Grinning, Genna went to the kitchen and returned minutes later with a tray of cake and tumblers of milk, to find Jared stretched out on the couch directly across from his daughter, sound asleep. Smiling, she went back to the kitchen to start supper.

Eight

"Holy Hannah!" Amy wailed. "You're still baking!"

"Good morning, Amy," Genna said sweetly without looking up from her task at the kitchen counter.

"What's he done now?" She maneuvered her pudgy body onto a stool at the counter.

"Who?" Genna refused to take the bait. This wasn't Jared's fault. Not directly anyway. His news that Simone Harcourt was going ahead with the custody suit had upset her more than she cared to say. How did the woman think she could prove Jared was an unfit parent? That question had nagged at the back of her mind since Jared had told her about this latest letter.

"Who? Houdini," Amy said sarcastically, popping open the can of diet Coke she'd brought along. "Who do you think?"

"Can't imagine."

"What are you making?" she asked suspiciously.

"Christmas cookies."

"It's the middle of summer!"

"Think of all the spare time I'll have at Christmas."

"Yeah, you'll have all kinds of spare time when they lock you up at the funny farm."

The back door banged open, saving Genna from any more of Amy's observations. "Delivery for Genna Hastings."

"Doesn't anybody knock anymore?" Genna questioned

as she wiped her hands on a dishtowel and pinned the delivery boy with a look. Then her eyes fell on the vase in his hands. It was a delicate milk-glass vase with a ruffled edge, and it was overflowing with violets and baby's breath.

Without another word Genna took it from him and went into the dining room, where she put the flowers on the table and slouched down on a chair to read the card.

For yesterday, when I needed you and you were there—J.J.

Amy handed the delivery boy two fresh Santa Claus cookies just as Genna burst into tears. The young man's eyes went huge with interest. Amy smacked him for staring and shooed him out the door. By the time she made it to the table, aching to hear a tearful true confession, Genna had reined in her emotions and gotten rid of the evidence of her outburst with a pink tissue. Amy grabbed for the card, but her friend held it out of reach. She scowled.

"They're from Jared," she accused the air. When Genna refused to answer, she slapped a chubby hand on the table and cackled like a crazed chicken, her dark eyes dancing. "I knew it! You *are* softening up! He's winning you over!"

"Baloney." If Amy was going to get an admission out of her, Genna was determined to have a little fun making her work for it.

"Ha! He sends you flowers and you burst into tears—"

"An allergic reaction."

"Yeah, sure. Allergic to telling the truth." She got on her knees on the Windsor chair and leaned across the table toward Genna, bracing her hands on the smooth wood surface. "Okay, Hastings, come clean—"

Bang. "Break out that new dress, Genna," sang a smoky sexy tenor. "I'm taking you dancing tonight."

"Blast you, Hennessy." Amy snarled at him. "She was just about to break!"

Jared took in the scene of Amy half on top of the table, her well-rounded backside sticking up in the air, and all sorts of weird explanations zinged through his brain.

Genna gave him a bland smile. "Yes, Amy was about to bring out her thumbscrews."

He bit the head off a reindeer cookie and chewed thoughtfully. "This sounds too kinky even for me. Is there some deep dark secret you're not telling me, Gen?"

"Why, yes . . . yes, there is." She smiled enigmatically, her eyes taking on a gleam of mischief she had seen so many times in Jared's. His gift had taken her by surprise, tilted her off balance. Now a rare burst of reckless abandon overpowered her, bringing her to her feet and propelling her toward the man.

It was Jared's turn to be shocked. And Amy wanted a confession? Well, why not give her one that would knock her socks off?

Suddenly wary, Jared took a step back, but Genna caught him, sliding her arms up around his neck. She gave him a sultry smile, tipped back his baseball cap, and kissed him full on the mouth.

Amy screamed.

Jared went through a rapid series of reactions—shock, followed by a swift involuntary rush of passion, then back to shock. Still hanging on to his mutilated reindeer cookie, he backed away from her, breaking lip contact at last.

"Gen-na!" he exclaimed as he turned red.

Genna grinned impishly and shrugged. "I love you."

Amy screamed again and staggered for the back door, fanning herself with a gingerbread man.

A smile twitching at her lips, Genna went to the sink and calmly started washing cookie sheets. She couldn't believe how good she felt now that she'd said it out loud. She loved Jared Hennessy. It felt doubly wonderful because he was none of the things she had forced herself to believe she wanted in a man. With Jared she would never wonder whether she had fallen for the man or his MBA. With Jared she had no doubts.

Except about the future.

She didn't know how much time she would have with him. She didn't know if he had welcomed her confession or cursed it. She had agreed to a no-strings relationship, yet she had come out and said she loved him. Well, that didn't mean she was expecting him to say it back. She was simply being honest. If he didn't like it . . .

Well, she decided determinedly, I won't think about that today. I'll think about that tomorrow. Nor would she think about the fact that Scarlett had ended up without Rhett while proclaiming tomorrow was another day. These were the eighties after all. A woman could have a summer romance if she wanted to.

Genna had never had a summer romance. She'd had summer jobs and had gone to summer school, but she'd never had a summer love. She'd been too practical and level-headed for that. Now she was thirty and for once she was going to throw practicality out the window. She was going to love Jared Hennessy for as long as she could, and when it was over, she wasn't going to have any regrets.

Jared sneaked his arms around her and snuggled up to her from behind. A shiver danced through Genna at the feel of her bottom tucked intimately against the most masculine part of him. She giggled as he nibbled at her neck. Apparently he had recovered from his attack of shyness now that Amy was gone.

"Do you realize it's been almost four whole days since we made love?" he queried against the sensitive flesh of her throat.

"Really? That long?" she quipped breathlessly, her bones turning to molasses.

His hips arched against her backside provocatively. Taking her earlobe between his teeth, he stated, "*That* long."

Genna gasped and groaned, dropping her dishrag into the sink with an audible plop. She braced her hands on the counter, her senses reeling.

"Bernice and Alyssa are making pasta. I'm told that takes a *long* time." His fingers slipped under the oversized pink T-shirt she wore and teased the undersides of her breasts.

"Long time . . ." The words fluttered from her lips

like butterflies. Lord, what this man could do to her body!

"You've never shown me the upstairs of your house, Genna," he purred, running the tip of his tongue down her throat while he circled a finger around each of her aching nipples. "I'll bet there's lots of interesting stuff up there."

"Mmmm. . . ."

"Why don't I lock the door and then you can show me?"

"Mmm."

How her rubber knees got her up the stairs, Genna wasn't sure. What she was sure of was that she wanted Jared with an intensity that robbed her of all coherent thought. And it was obvious he felt the same way. If their lovemaking had been unhurried the first time, this time it was anything but.

They made it to the general vicinity of Genna's white iron bed before they found each other's arms. They met in a blaze of passion and urgency. Tongues dueled as eager hands tore at buttons and zippers. Genna's baggy jeans hit the floor and she kicked out of them as they went down on the bed in a tangle of arms and legs.

"I want you," Jared moaned hotly against her mouth. He pulled her legs up around his bare hips and thrust into her without preamble.

The excitement of sudden need had been their foreplay. Genna was more than ready for him. She ran her hands down his back, arching against him wantonly, savoring the satin heat of their union.

Jared watched her for a moment. Beneath him Genna was the most beautiful creature on earth. She gave herself to him so freely, without hesitation or reservation or coyness. She loved him. A shudder went through him. This was what he needed to make his life complete, for this woman to love him.

Another shudder rolled through his body, reminding him of his hunger for Genna. Her eyes fluttered open and locked with his as they moved together in passion's dance, as they raced together toward passion's edge and hurled themselves over it.

With her name on his lips Jared dropped his head to her shoulder and collapsed on top of her. They were half on the bed and half off, and he weighed a ton, lying on top of her, but Genna didn't care. She felt wonderfully complete and content in a way she had never experienced before. *I love him.*

"Did you mean it, Gen?" he asked in that smoky voice that turned her blood hot and heavy in her veins. He raised up on one elbow and looked deep into her eyes.

"I love you," she said simply, acutely aware of how vulnerable she was to his rejection. There was every chance that he wouldn't want her to admit being so involved. She started to open her mouth to tell him he didn't have to worry, that she was a big girl and she could handle a short-term relationship. But he banished the noble speech from her mind with a tender kiss.

A slow, sweet smile curved his mouth. He brushed her tangled hair back from her face and tugged her T-shirt up. Keeping their bodies joined, Jared bent his head and leisurely attended to her breasts with his mouth, kissing, sucking, laving.

Genna moaned with delight. A tide of renewed desire surged through her, stronger than the one that had swept her upstairs in the first place. It gushed through her arms and legs, fingers and toes. It settled like a whirlpool in her breast, the sensations swirling around and around as Jared's tongue swirled around and around. Then his warm lips closed on the turgid tip and he sucked urgently.

Genna's fingers dug into his short black hair. The sensations shot to the pit of her belly, and she tightened around him. She felt him stir inside her again. He moved against her in short, teasing strokes that drove her crazy.

'You're so damn sexy," he said with a growl, nipping at her collarbone then kissing where he'd bitten.

Sexy. The word didn't even begin to describe the way he made her feel. What happened to her when she made love with Jared went well beyond the realm of

Genna's meager experience. She lost all control of her mind and body and was swept away weightlessly on waves of sensual abandon.

He rolled them over on the creaking old bed so he was on his back and Genna was sprawled on top of him. He took his fill of her mouth then gently pushed her back.

"Sit up, baby," he ordered hoarsely.

Genna obeyed, groaning deep in her throat as she took him deeper inside her.

Jared bit his lip and forced himself to be still. "Take your top off, sweetheart."

She did as he asked, and he shuddered with desire as he watched her pull the pink T-shirt over her head, her full, ripe breasts thrusting up as she arched her back. The shirt cast over a chair and forgotten, she turned her gaze, dark and glazed with passion, back to Jared. His breath caught in his throat as she began to move on him.

She moved slowly, all her attention focused on the special, warm, silken pocket nature had left her just for him, as he filled her. Her head rolled back, eyes closed, her dark lashes curving along the line of her cheek.

He braced his feet on the bed, dimly aware that he was still wearing his sneakers. He gritted his teeth, fighting the completion that rushed toward him. Reaching out, he caught Genna's hand and drew it to the dewy valley where their bodies were joined. Her eyes flew open and she gasped his name as the explosion of fulfillment shook both her body and his.

"I love you, Genna," he whispered, pulling her down on top of him.

They lay in a happy, contented, exhausted tangle of limbs. Jared stroked a hand over the curve of Genna's hip the way he might stroke a cat. He loved the feel of her, soft and smooth with just a little extra padding in all the right places. A smile of utter serenity graced his handsome features as he opened his eyes to gaze into

Genna's. They shared her pillow. It had a hand-embroidered pillowcase and smelled of potpourri and summer and Genna.

"You're so beautiful," he whispered, too exhausted to do more.

She smiled like a pixy and giggled. "I'm not beautiful. I'm cute."

He found the strength to chuckle. "Adorable."

Snuggling her closer and pressing a kiss to her unruly mop of waves, he let his eyes take in the details of the loft bedroom. It was like Genna—not too big, but very feminine; an endearing mix of practicality and whimsy. Every piece of furniture looked like a flea market refugee, most if it repainted white and adorned with old patchwork pillows, porcelain figurines, and beribboned bouquets of dried flowers. He guessed this would be her hideaway, the place where she would come to read romance novels and fashion magazines, though she would probably never admit it.

So tied up in being sensible. He wondered if she had ever let herself be free of responsibility, childlike, footloose. Had Genna ever done anything just to be crazy? He doubted it. Probably since childhood she had worked her fanny off to be as unlike her father as possible. Jared imagined that admitting to being in love with him the way she had was the most reckless thing she'd ever done. It meant a lot to him. Practical, level-headed Genna confessing love for an . . . individual . . . like himself. And in front of a witness no less. He was, after all, the antithesis of her ideal man.

He was tempted to tell her how much it meant to him, how much *she* meant to him, but he forced himself to hold back. Genna hadn't wanted a relationship with him in the first place. He'd be a fool to push her now, when she was only just beginning to accept this very special magic that they shared. For Genna's sake he would be patient. For Genna he would do just about anything. Jared grinned and stretched, feeling incredibly self-satisfied.

"Thank you for the flowers," Genna said, running her foot up and down his muscular calf. They had finally managed to get his jeans and shoes off. Lord, how she loved the feel of his body. He was so solid, and he was solid in more than the physical sense. A woman couldn't ask for a better man, a better friend or lover. She was determined to enjoy every minute she had with him.

"You're welcome. And thank you for helping."

"Did you get everything straightened out with Alyssa?"

"Mmm-hmm. We had a good talk last night. I think it's all straightened out. I know I need to understand that she's going to miss her mother. I guess I'm just touchy about it because I was always jealous of the time Elaine got to spend with her. Between that and this thing with Simone . . ."

Genna reached up to run her fingertips down the taught plane of his cheek. She could feel a muscle working in his jaw. "Didn't your lawyer say there's nothing to worry about? You're Alyssa's natural father and, thanks to me," she teased, "well on your way to becoming a model citizen."

"I know, I know. There's just . . . something. I don't know."

Just something. Genna didn't tell him she felt it too. She shivered a little and made a show of pulling the sheet up over her bare shoulders.

"I just feel as though she's got some kind of trick play up her sleeve, something my defense isn't ready for." He patted Genna's bottom and forced a grin. "Listen to me. Here I am, talking like a quarterback, and I don't have to leave for training camp for another two weeks."

"That soon?" Genna cursed herself a jillion times for blurting that out. She didn't want him to feel as if she were tying unwanted strings to their relationship. He was hers for the summer. He hadn't indicated he wanted anything more serious than that, and she wouldn't make the mistake of assuming he did. Nor would she try pushing him into it. She'd done that once; she had the emotional scars to prove it. If loving him meant letting him go, then that was exactly what she'd do.

Misinterpreting her sudden stiffness for plain old

embarrassment, Jared chuckled. He tipped her chin up, giving her his teasing grin. "Gen-na, are you gonna miss me?"

She twisted a wry smile up at the corner of her mouth, but couldn't quite meet his gaze. "Don't flatter yourself, Hennessy."

"You're a cruel woman, Genna Hastings." He laughed, rolling over so he was on his hands and knees, straddling her. "So, are you going dancing with me tonight, or what?"

"Dancing?" Genna asked, as if the concept were totally unknown to her. She couldn't seem to tear her gaze or her mind off the massive male form looming over her.

"Yeah, you know, cut the rug, trip the light fantastic. Dance. It's a social activity."

"Oh. Dance," she said stupidly, her gaze feasting on the scenery of his thickset chest and tapering waist. His belly was flat and ridged with muscle, and a thin line of downy brown hair bisected it and ran in a widening path to a thicket of curls around his—

"I'd love to, doll," he teased, not missing the trail her darkening eyes took, "but I don't want to spoil you."

A vivid blush stained Genna's cheeks. She shoved him off the bed with a strategically placed hand and sat up, reaching for her pink T-shirt. "You're impossibly conceited."

Jared bounced to his feet, pulling on his underwear. "Might as well face it, babe," he said, amused, "you're addicted."

Otis "Boo Boo" Paige took up the floor space of a family of four. He made Jared look like a munchkin. He was the biggest, meanest-looking man Genna had ever laid eyes on. She did a strangulation number on her black satin clutch purse as she stood in Jared's living room looking up—up—up at the man, her features frozen in an expression that was a mixture of cordiality and stark terror.

Jared introduced him as "the baddest offensive lineman in the cosmos"—Genna assumed that was a compliment—then the men slapped hands, butted heads, and pretended to shoot each other with finger pistols.

Jared searched his cluttered rolltop desk for his car keys. Debris scattered this way and that. It looked to Genna as if someone had emptied a Hefty bag of crumpled papers onto the surface. How he ever found anything there was a miracle, she thought. Who knew what lurked under all that rubble. Someday he'd probably come across the Holy Grail.

"Boo Boo's going to baby-sit Lyssa while we're out," Jared said, still digging.

"Nnnn," Genna said through her teeth, raising her brows.

"I'm not a baby," Alyssa protested, swinging her legs over the edge of the desk chair.

Outlandish as the thought was, still Genna was tempted to suggest taking the little girl along, then Boo Boo smiled and his whole tough-guy image shattered. Suddenly he possessed all the deadly menace of a teddy bear. His eyes glowed a soft velvet brown. He had a space between his two front teeth and talked with a slight lisp.

"It's a pleasure to meet you, Miss Hastings." His voice was like cotton candy.

"Boo's got his master's in child development."

Why should that surprise me, Genna asked herself. She offered Boo Boo her hand and her smile. "Nice to meet you, Mr. Paige. Jared's friends are always so full of surprises."

Otis laughed his understanding.

"Daddy, Genna's got her new dress on," Alyssa said from her seat in the swivel chair. With a wink Jared swung her up in his arms, and nose to nose they sang a jazzy number about a woman in a fancy dress out for a night on the town.

Boo Boo shook his head. "The man is crazy."

"So I've noticed," Genna said with a grin.

Jared swung his daughter over to her baby-sitter,

and she scrambled like a monkey onto Paige's mountain-range shoulders.

"Be a good girl for Uncle Boo Boo, Lyss," Jared said, taking Genna by the elbow and steering her toward the door. "And don't win all his pennies away from him."

"The lady plays a mean Go Fish," Boo Boo informed Genna.

They strolled arm in arm down the sidewalk toward Jared's gleaming black Corvette. Around them the summer evening settled into a warm golden haze. Down the block Theron Ralston, in checkered Bermuda shorts and dress shoes, polished his yard jockey while Mrs. Ralston's poodle slipped around the back side of the statue and lifted its leg.

"Did I tell you, Miss Hastings, that you look like Christmas and my birthday all wrapped up in a million bucks in that dress?"

Genna blushed.

That wicked Jack Nicholson grin slashed across his face as he corralled her between his arms and the car. "Why, Miss Hastings, one might assume you are unaccustomed to male praise."

"One might be correct," she said with syrupy sweetness. "But one needn't look so smug."

"One can't help it when one thinks of all the bozos that have missed the boat here." He touched a feather-light kiss to her lips, trying to be careful not to smudge her lipstick.

Genna reached a forefinger up to erase a telltale trace of red from his lower lip. He had the most incredibly sensuous mouth, she thought, tingles snaking up her arm and down to the tips of her toes. There was always a smile lurking around the corners of it, a smile that could be boyish, devilish, or all-out sexy.

She looked up into his baby-blue eyes, loving every inch of him. This wasn't the first time a man had taken her dancing, but no man had ever done it with such style.

Jared had promised her she would wear the elegant, extravagant purple taffeta dress, and so she was. She felt like a princess. She felt on-top-of-the-world beautiful, with a twinge of embarrassed shyness. Couldn't people tell by looking at her that she was more preppy than princess?

Jared shook his head as if he'd read her thoughts.

"Did I tell you, Mr. Hennessy, that you look incredibly dapper tonight?" she asked.

His shoulders just tested the seams of a dazzling white dinner jacket. The wing collar of his white shirt squared off the lines of his strong jaw. A neatly tied black bow tie resided above a row of shiny black studs that marched down his chest. Black Italian leather shoes, the cost of which probably made Genna's car payment look like pin money, stood beneath a stylishly cut pair of black trousers.

Jared grinned. "You like me all dolled up, Teach?"

"Don't let it go to your head, Hennessy."

"I could change into a T-shirt if this is too much for you. Someone just sent me one from Chowderhead's Chowderhouse—"

"That's okay," she said dryly, her hands smoothing down his lapels. "You know you had me believing you didn't own a shirt with buttons, much less a suit."

"No." He shook his head, sliding his arms around her waist. "You had yourself believing that, Miss Typecaster."

She smiled at his smile as he lowered his mouth toward hers. Suddenly a flashbulb exploded to Genna's right, almost sending her on top of the Corvette.

"Heaven above, Amy! What are you trying to do, give us heart attacks?" Genna squealed.

"Did you get my good side?" Jared asked, mugging for the camera.

Amy grinned unrepentently and saluted them with her Instamatic camera. "Just capturing the moment, as they say. You kids have a good time now." She adjusted the small black bow in Genna's hair.

"Yes, Mom," Genna droned, rolling her eyes. "Don't wait up; some of us kids are going for sodas after the prom."

• • •

Genna wasn't sure what she had been expecting when Jared had said they were going dancing. A modern, ultra-chic discotheque, she supposed. What she got was old-fashioned elegance with a capital E.

Copper Beeches was a turn-of-the-century mansion named for the trees that lined the drive. It had been built with a lavish hand by an early railroad baron who had wanted to make all his filthy rich Hartford neighbors pea green with envy. The family had died out in the forties, and the grand old house had been left more or less to its own devices until some enterprising businesswoman had bought it and turned it into a posh hotel.

The floors were polished marble and parquet, the walls covered with gilt-framed oil paintings, the tall windows hung with silks and velvets. The grand ballroom was something straight out of *The Great Gatsby.* It was done in gold and white, and it had a dance floor that gleamed like glass. At one end of the room a tuxedoed orchestra played romantic songs from the twenties and thirties. Couples in elegant evening attire danced or sat at linen-draped tables sipping champagne from crystal flutes.

Genna was in a daze. She was sure her heels never touched the floor as Jared led her in on his arm, receiving respectful nods from the staff. She'd have sworn the champagne she drank was liquid stars, the music filling her head from some faraway dream. Until Jared pulled her into his arms on the dance floor, she didn't quite believe any of it was real.

"Surprised?" he asked.

"Endlessly," Genna answered. It seemed she couldn't resign herself to the fact that she would never know what to expect from this man. She was a person who had always needed control over her life. With Jared she felt as if she were on a galloping horse with no bridle; the ride was exhilarating, but a little frightening.

The gravel-edged rumble of sexy male laughter sounded low in Jared's throat. "You have to stop trying to pigeonhole me, princess. Just lean back and enjoy the ride."

"I would if I could just shake this feeling that any minute now the cook is going to come out and tell me I have to go wash the glasses," she quipped.

"Is that your own version of *Cinderella*?"

"Yep. *Gennarella*, I call it."

"Well, never fear, Gennarella, your devastatingly handsome prince isn't about to let you out of his arms."

"Are you sure there's room for me? That ego of yours takes up a lot of space," she teased.

She could have danced all night. She could easily have spent the next eon or so in Jared's arms, his body swaying smoothly with hers. The man took cheek-to-cheek literally and occasionally allowed his smooth, warm lips to make taste-testing forays down her cheek and along her jawline to her lips as they danced. He held her close, singing the old standards in her ear in his velvet-soft voice.

The only small damper on their evening came with the last song. A red-haired woman with enormous black eyes and a shimmering silver flapper dress took her place at the microphone and began singing a song about a woman whose love is leaving her and who doesn't know what she'll do after he's gone.

The song went straight to Genna's vulnerable heart. Jared was leaving for training camp in two weeks. Then it would be fall and the football season would start. What would become of their summer love? She burrowed closer to him. She swore to herself she wouldn't push him for more than they already had. They had a good friendship, and she would content herself with that. Jared had told her he loved her, but she knew from experience how fickle a phrase that was when uttered by a man in the throes of passion.

When the song ended, Jared tipped her head up and kissed her deeply, a kiss that offered a taste of heaven, one that she drank in to soothe her uncertain heart.

He lifted his mouth a few inches from hers. "If we didn't have a baby-sitter waiting, I'd take you upstairs and we could make a perfect end to a perfect evening."

Visions of satin sheets and carved mahogany furnishings drifted through Genna's head. Visions of the two of them naked on those sheets, with her in Jared's powerful embrace and Jared telling her over and over how much he loved her and needed her—for all time, not just for the summer. She didn't even recognize the desperation in her voice when she said, "Another time, maybe?"

He brushed a hand over her bouncy hair, his heart full of love for her as she stood against him and gazed up at him with her bottomless blue eyes so full of longing and something achingly close to sadness. Was she that afraid of a long-term relationship with him? How long was it going to take before he had her complete trust? He traced the outline of her softly parted lips with his forefinger and said, "Another time, definitely."

Nine

Just like in *Cinderella*, the clock struck, and their fantasy evening was over. And it struck with a vengeance. Simone Harcourt was waiting for them in Jared's living room.

Genna knew who the woman was before anyone said anything. As soon as they'd stepped in the door Jared had gone utterly still. Genna could feel the tension emanating from him. For one long moment the entire room was held frozen in a terrible sense of suspended animation as Jared and Simone stared at each other with hatred in their eyes.

Finally Otis rose from his chair and came toward them. "Hope you had a nice time," he said, moving toward the door. The implication was that if they hadn't already had a good time, they weren't going to start now. "Alyssa was a sweetheart, as always. She went to bed at eight-thirty, but I don't believe she's sleeping very well now." He shot a pointed look at Jared's ex–sister-in-law before giving her a stiff bow. His voice frosted over as he said, "It was a pleasure meeting you, Ms. Harcourt."

The woman merely nodded.

Genna thought Simone was as lovely and cold as an ice sculpture. She sat on a beige wing chair with her back as straight as a post and her elegant hands folded on her lap. She was in her late thirties, Genna guessed, with neat short black hair and flawless makeup on patrician features. Her tailored tan business suit suggested an angular, slender body. The legs crossed beneath her pencil-thin skirt were long and graceful.

As soon as Boo Boo was out the door, Jared broke their staredown. "Simone," he said in a voice so cold it gave Genna the shivers. With a hand on the small of her back, Jared brought her farther into the room with him.

"I should have known you wouldn't be here when I arrived," the woman said accusingly.

Jared's eyes burned her with a baleful glare. "I'm supposed to feel guilty when you didn't have the common courtesy to call and warn me you were coming?"

She looked away, knowing she was being unreasonable. It was to her advantage to put him on the defensive. "I see you've been out partying as usual. What cheap dives are you frequenting these days, Jared?"

A muscle twitched in his cheek. "Genna and I have been at Copper Beeches. It's the first time I've gone anywhere in two months. Not that it's any of your business."

He was dangerously close to losing his temper, Genna thought, biting her lip. It wouldn't do for him to lose his cool when the woman was in perfect control and obviously baiting him. Genna put her hand on Jared's forearm. It was like iron beneath his dinner jacket.

"Jared," she murmured. "Introduce me."

He looked at her as though she'd just materialized from out of nowhere. Realization dawned slowly, softening the fierceness of his features.

"Genna, Simone Harcourt. I've told you *all* about her." He shot a meaningful look at the composed Ms. Harcourt. "Simone, this is Genna Hastings, my neighbor—"

"How convenient for you." Simone smiled unpleasantly.

"And friend," he bit off, his face turning to granite, his eyes twin blue flames. He was about to say something more—or perhaps go for the woman's throat—but Genna cut him off at the pass.

"So," she said, stepping forward with a saccharine smile. "You're the poor lonely woman trying to steal Jared's daughter from him. How incredibly rude of you to drop by. I was under the mistaken impression that Elaine's family was well bred. Well, no matter. I'll go make us some coffee, though I seriously doubt Jared will invite you to stay."

She turned from Simone, smiled and winked at Jared. A suspicious twitch tugged at the corner of his mouth. He watched Genna sweep from the room like a queen. She had rescued him from making a major tactical error and reminded him he wasn't in this dogfight alone. They were a team.

Sliding his hands casually into his pants pockets, Jared turned back to Simone, who looked considerably less composed than she had a moment ago.

"Genna will be Alyssa's kindergarten teacher this fall. She's been a tremendous help in getting Alyssa to cope with her mother's death. She minored in psychology and graduated summa cum laude from Vassar."

Simone swallowed. Things were not going the way she had expected. She hadn't been expecting Jared's neat, tastefully decorated home or quiet, colonial Tory Hills, with its treelined streets. She hadn't been expecting a baby-sitter who looked as if he could crush beer cans by scowling at them but instead spent the evening regaling her with the details of his master's thesis: The Importance of Paternal Involvement in Child Rearing. She hadn't expected the station wagon in the garage or the swing set in the fenced backyard.

A headache began to throb between her neatly plucked brows. Jared was nothing like she'd remembered. Her sister had married an overgrown teenager with long hair and an I-don't-give-a-damn attitude. The man standing before her appeared to be mature. He was composed, sardonic, and handsomely turned out. The diamond stud in his ear gave him the dangerous aura of a gentleman pirate from a bygone era.

And then there was Genna Hastings. Summa cum laude from Vassar? That blasted private investigator had told her Genna Hastings was unemployed. She should have known better than to hire a man who looked like a bargain-basement Mike Hammer. From the pictures he'd taken, she had come to the erroneous conclusion that Genna Hastings was a topless dancer, or worse.

"What are you doing here, Simone?" Jared asked in a bored tone as he leaned indolently back against his cluttered desk.

With a deep breath she calmed her features and her mind. She had to keep her objective in clear view. "I came here to give you a chance to settle this business out of court. I think we both know what will be best for Alyssa in the long run. There's really no need to drag your personal dirty laundry into public; your reputation is bad enough already. Turn Alyssa over to my care, and I'll be very generous with your visitation privileges."

Jared gave an unamused bark of laughter. "That's big of you, considering you don't have squat to take to court."

"Don't I?" She arched an elegant brow at Jared, then gave Genna, who had just returned to the room, an insulting once-over. She rose gracefully from the chair with a large manila envelope in her hand and came toward them, taking her time. She had the moment and she was making the most of it. She stroked the envelope lovingly, her confidence returning. "I think the court will find these extremely interesting. Proof positive in black and white that you aren't fit to have Alyssa in your custody. Really, they only substantiate the less than desirable reputation you've built for yourself over the years."

She handed the envelope to Jared and stood back to watch.

A feeling of foreboding crawled over Genna as she watched Jared's hands open the flap and extract Simone's "proof." Then the world abruptly dropped out from under her.

The envelope was full of grainy eight-by-ten black and white blowups of Jared and herself. Several had been shot from outside the back screen door of Genna's own house. Those were of Jared holding her on his lap on the kitchen floor. There was one of them nose to nose in the department store on the day they'd run into Allan Corrigan.

The great majority of the photos had been taken from outside Jared's bedroom window. The horizontal slashes of venetian blinds cutting across the pictures, only added to the feeling of voyeurism. And though the quality of the photographs was poor, the subject matter was quite easily defined: she and Jared undressing each other, naked, embracing, making love.

Genna felt sick. Bile rose in her throat. What kind of monster could do this? Someone she didn't even know had taken her cherished memories and reduced them to pornography. Tears blurred her vision. She felt her knees sag as if the bones were suddenly disintegrating. Jared's arm came around her bare back as strong as an oak limb. He held her against a solid body that trembled with rage.

"I'm sorry, baby," he whispered, kissing her hair. He turned his eyes on Simone then, and she stepped back at the pure, violent hatred in them. "Want to take a picture of this too, Simone?"

She flinched at the acid in his voice. Her veneer of confidence had cracked the moment Genna had laid eyes on the pictures. She had looked so hurt, so betrayed. That wasn't at all what Simone had expected. Anger, yes, and embarrassment, but Genna had reacted as if something beautiful had just been senselessly destroyed.

Jared eased Genna down onto his desk chair, where she sat in numb, shocked silence. Everything had taken on a sense of unreality for her. She felt stupid and helpless in her fancy party dress.

Jared wished he could do something to ease Genna's pain, but the only thing he could think of was to wrap his hands around Simone Harcourt's throat and choke the life out of her. He could take what Simone dished out to him personally, but she had hurt Genna, who was an innocent bystander in all this. That was unforgivable.

He rounded on Simone, feeling sick and disgusted,

swinging at her with the envelope and photographs clutched in his hand. "You bitch! You pay someone to take pictures like this and you think *I'm* not fit to be a parent?"

Simone swallowed convulsively, raking a badly shaking hand through her dark hair. "The court needs evidence—"

"Evidence!" he shouted. "What the hell kind of evidence is this? Evidence that Genna and I are two healthy adults who care very much for each other? You don't see Alyssa in these pictures, do you? *Do you*?"

"N-no—but—" she stammered.

"She wasn't even in the damn house!"

Trembling, Simone grabbed the back of a chair for support as she watched Jared pace the room like a caged panther. Never in her life had she seen such blind fury. It terrified her to know she was the one guilty of unleashing it, terrified that it might turn full tide on her.

Jared stopped his pacing, his chest heaving beneath his elegant evening wear. Hands shaking with rage, he shoved the photographs back into the envelope and resealed it. For a long moment he stood there, the air around him vibrating with the same anticipation that thickens the air before a violent storm.

Suddenly he swore viciously and flung the envelope to his desktop, sending papers flying. His hands ravaged his short raven hair, and he cradled his head in them as he struggled to rein in his emotions. When he spoke, a fault line of possessive desperation cracked through his rough voice. "What kind of evidence am I supposed to find that shows how much I love my daughter?"

His question hung in the air.

Genna saw his eyes glaze with tears and she looked away, her heart breaking for him. Standing in the doorway was Alyssa, barefoot and looking very tiny in her eyelet nightgown. Her big eyes swam with tears as she clutched her doll to her.

"Daddy?"

Jared was on his knees beside her instantly, smoothing a hand back over her neatly braided black hair. "What is it, baby?"

"Why are you fighting?" One lone tear skittered down her cheek.

Jared tenderly took his daughter in his arms and brushed the tear away with his thumb. He had been on the verge of losing every vestige of self-control; now he struggled to regain it. Alyssa was frightened, she needed his strength now, his reassurance. "It's nothing, sweetheart. Aunt Simone and I are having a disagreement, that's all. It's nothing for you to worry about, muffin."

Alyssa looked from adult to adult, clearly skeptical of her father's explanation. A little whimper came from her throat as she cuddled against Jared. "I'm scared, Daddy."

Not half as scared as I am. I love you so much, he thought as he hugged all forty-two pounds of sweet-smelling little girl and rained kisses over her dark head. *God, don't let me lose her now.*

"There's nothing to be scared of, baby. Everything will be all right, I promise," he muttered, immediately feeling like a fraud and a liar. "You should be in bed, muffin; it's late. Let's go, okay?"

"Come and tuck me and Dollie in, Daddy," Alyssa insisted, dropping her head to his broad shoulder and sticking her thumb into her mouth.

"Sure thing, sweetheart."

They disappeared down the hall, leaving Genna and Simone and a deafening silence. Genna would have sat there for the rest of her life without speaking. She wanted to pretend Simone Harcourt didn't exist, hadn't violated her love for Jared, wasn't trying to take Alyssa away. She had tried to temper her feelings with some sense of sympathy toward the woman. Simone had lost her sister; having Alyssa with her was the one way of holding on to some part of Elaine. But the ability to think objectively had shriveled and died inside Genna, and she sat quietly running her palms over the skirt of her dress.

The pressure of guilt forced Simone to speak. "I want only what's best for Alyssa. She's my sister's child."

"She's Jared's child," Genna said with weary vehemence.

Simone went to the wing chair to retrieve her beige calfskin purse. She took an uneven breath and shook her head as she dug for the keys to her car. "He's not the man I remember."

Genna wanted to laugh. Simone had been expecting a cocky quarterback with punk hair and a T-shirt from Chowderhead's Chowderhouse, as if that had anything to do with the man Jared Hennessy was inside. She could almost sympathize with the woman's confusion. Almost. "Maybe you just never looked close enough."

If Simone had meant to make a grand exit, Genna didn't wait to see it. She kicked her heels off and padded out of the room in her stocking feet. It was late and she was tired, the kind of bone-deep tired that comes after a highly charged emotional battle. She couldn't help but wonder who had won.

At the door to Alyssa's room she stopped and leaned against the frame, hesitating. The door was ajar. Her need to see Jared overriding her respect for his privacy, she pushed it open with one finger and peered in.

Alyssa was asleep, curled on her side with her thumb in her mouth and Dollie tucked securely beneath her chin. Jared knelt beside the bed, head bowed as if in prayer as he watched his daughter sleep.

He must have sensed Genna standing there, because she didn't move, yet Jared turned to stare at her. With the weariness of a hundred-year-old man, he got to his feet and moved across the room. He had tugged loose his bow tie, and it hung like a ribbon of black silk around the open neck of his wing collar.

"Had enough excitement for one evening?" he asked in a throaty whisper, one corner of his mouth lifting fractionally.

"I'm okay." She sighed. She reached out and fingered a black stud on his shirtfront.

His gaze held fragments of respect, wonder, something more. Finally he said, "Yeah, you are."

"Are you?"

It seemed to take an eternity for him to gather the strength to shrug. "Don't worry about me. I can play with pain." He forced a pathetically fake grin. "That's why I make the big bucks."

Genna didn't smile back. "Don't bother with the act, Hennessy. We're a team, remember?"

He heaved a sigh and ran the tip of his forefinger down Genna's upturned nose. "I remember. If I'd known how rough this game was going to get when I recruited you, I'd have warned you, you know."

"I know. I wouldn't have done anything differently. I don't have any regrets. I'm a big girl."

"I've noticed." The glimmer of a twinkle lit his eyes in the dim light of the hallway. His hands found her waist and he drew her close. "Listen, I don't have a game ball to award you, but I'll buy you a drink. You don't mind using Bullwinkle tumblers, do you?"

"What?" she teased. "No Rocky the Flying Squirrel?"

"Sorry. The burger joint's not offering those until next week."

With tired smiles on their faces they walked to the kitchen arm in arm for support.

By silent agreement the subject of Simone was dropped. Conspicuous by her absence, they assumed she had taken her evidence and gone home, leaving them alone to sit on the patio holding hands, sipping fine Irish whiskey and listening to the quiet sounds of the night.

"Rise and whine, Sleeping Beauty," a smoky voice murmured in Genna's ear. She lay sprawled on her stomach in bed with her nightgown hitched up around her waist and her face buried in her pillow.

"Oven mitts," she mumbled, squirming into a more comfortable position.

"Oven mitts?" Jared said. He stood back a moment to survey the situation—and the view. He'd had every intention of waking Genna quickly; he was eager to get on the road. But when he'd come up the stairs and seen her enchanting backside presented so invitingly, his intentions had gone out the window. A man couldn't really pass up an opportunity like this, now, could he? he asked himself.

He pulled off his cowboy boots, dropping them on the rag rug beside the bed, then tried to ease down onto the bed beside Genna. She was taking up too much space and wouldn't budge. "Hey, bed hog," he teased in her ear. "Move over."

One sleepy eye opened and focused on him, and she smiled. She made enough room on the bed for him to settle comfortably, then immediately cuddled up to him and sighed contentedly. In her foggy mind she never thought to wonder what he was doing in her bed or how he had gotten into her house. The important thing was he was here, and it seemed very right.

"Hi," she said in a sleep-rusty voice which Jared found incredibly sexy.

"Hi yourself, gorgeous." He smiled. Her hair was all mussed around her head, and she had raccoon smudges of mascara beneath the bleary blue orbs of her eyes. He thought she was adorable. "You awake?"

"Mmmm-hmmm." Her hands began to wander over the vast planes of his chest but stopped abruptly. She looked up and frowned at him. "You're wearing clothes," she said accusingly.

Jared chuckled. He pulled her head down for a long, hungry kiss as one hand explored every inch of exposed flesh from waist to thigh. His fingers combed through the soft, dark curls that protected her femininity, and he teased her until she was gasping for air.

"Yes, I'm wearing clothes," he whispered silkily. "Want me to take them off?"

Her hands were already unbuckling his belt. "Let's just rearrange them. I'm in kind of a hurry."

"Really?" he remarked dryly as he rose so she could yank his jeans and briefs down. "I hadn't noticed."

"Quit fooling around, Hennessy," she groused, her fingers delighting in the feel of his skin.

Jared refrained from pointing out that fooling around

seemed to be exactly what she wanted to do. Instead, he rolled her over and made love to her with an enthusiasm she more than matched.

The moment of sweet, hot release came quickly, but seemed to go on and on. Slowly, gasps relaxed into sighs that slid into even breathing. Just as Genna was drifting off, Jared pinched her bottom.

"Jared," she exclaimed as if she had just noticed him. "What are you doing here?"

"That should have been self-explanatory," he said, nuzzling behind her ear. "Maybe I'm not doing it right."

"I wouldn't worry on that score if I were you." Her body was still tingling from his touch. He made her feel wonderful . . . and sleepy. Her eyes drifted shut.

"I came to wake you up," he explained, disgustingly chipper. "We're going on a trip."

"Hmmm? Wake up? What time is it?"

He glanced out the window. "Dawn."

"Funny, I didn't hear it crack," she grumbled, burying her face deeper into her pillow.

"Well, you were . . . preoccupied." He chuckled, sliding out of bed and straightening his clothes. "Come on, get up! We've got places to go, things to do!"

"Go?" Genna rolled to her back and looked at him with only one eye open. "Go where?"

"Up to the Berkshires," he said as if she should have known. "An old friend of mine has a farm up there. We're going to spend the day."

She sat up, watching him dig through her dresser drawers for clothes. He tossed her a black lace bra, a pair of plum tap pants, and two mismatched socks. "When did you decide this?"

"A couple of hours ago." He lifted a cream satin negligee out of a drawer by one strap and raised an eyebrow. "It's all set up. I called him."

Genna glanced at the clock. It wasn't quite six. "And he's still your friend?"

"Don't you own any boots?" he asked, bent over in her closet. Shoes came flying out in all directions.

Genna popped out of bed, hooked a finger through a

belt loop on his jeans, and pulled him out of her closet. "I can dress myself, thank you. If I let you pick out my clothes, I'll be on Mr. Blackwell's list, right up there with Cyndi Lauper."

He sat on the bed and watched her as if he thought she might need help.

"Where's Alyssa?" she asked, pulling on a plaid cotton shirt.

"On your couch, sound asleep. She never wakes up before seven."

"Such an intelligent child," she said, casting a look of longing at her rumpled bed. It had been almost three before she had crawled into it. "So unlike her father."

As she buttoned her blouse, the question she should have asked first popped into her head. "How did you get into my house?"

"Mastercard," he replied with a perfectly straight face. "We've got to get you a deadbolt lock, Gen. You never know when some sex fiend is going to let himself in here and help himself to the goodies."

She gave him a look. "Right."

They drove up into the beautiful Berkshire Hills of western Massachusetts, Alyssa and Genna sleeping most of the way. When they finally stopped, they were at a farm that looked as if it belonged on a scenic calendar. There was a pristine white farmhouse and red outbuildings nestled into the side of an emerald green hill, with woods stretching beyond the pastures.

Jared's friend, Will McDonal, had been a teammate for several years, until an injury had forced him to retire. He was a big blond man with a quiet manner and a pleasant grin. Neither he nor his pretty, dark-haired wife, Kelly, seemed the least surprised or upset by Jared's early morning call. Apparently they knew Jared well enough to expect the unexpected, Genna thought.

Jared, Alyssa, and Genna spent most of the day riding horseback on the trails that crisscrossed the woods of the McDonal farm. Alyssa rode in the saddle in front of her father. Jared had politely refused Kelly's offer to baby-sit, an action that gave Genna a clue as to what this excursion was all about.

Jared wanted to spend time with his daughter. Quiet, special time. Although he refused to say one word about it, Simone's visit had upset him a lot, Genna thought as she watched him point out a deer to Alyssa. This was his way of getting away from the problem and hoarding memories . . . just in case.

It was supposed to be a relaxing day. Jared was anything but relaxed, though he tried to give a convincing performance. He was wound tighter than the proverbial spring. Genna could see it in the set of his shoulders, the falseness of his grin. She sensed it in his every movement, tasted it in his kiss. They picnicked on a blanket in an open meadow and, while Alyssa napped, Jared took Genna in his arms and kissed her with the desperation of a starving man let loose at a feast.

Genna made no comment on his behavior. Nor did she try to get him to talk about it. She stayed close to him, offering her nearness, her touch, her quiet support and friendship, knowing that was more comfort to him now than any words she might have said.

They came home that night to find Bernice still at Jared's house even though it was past seven in the evening.

"Bernice, what are you doing here?" Jared whispered as he carried in a sleeping Alyssa.

The housekeeper held up an ivory envelope. "This came special delivery, boss. I wanted to make sure you got it. I wasn't about to leave it on that disaster area you call a desk."

Genna watched Jared lay his daughter on the couch and take the letter from Bernice with a hand that wasn't quite steady. For a long moment he just stared at it, his face unusually pale. Finally he opened the envelope and extracted the letter.

Jared's eyes scanned the neatly typed missive, the hard knot of fear in his chest slowly unfurling into ribbons of joy. Relief washed over him, leaving him weak and trembling. His shout of triumph escaped before he could even finish reading the letter, but he had seen the important part, the part that said Simone felt she had been terribly wrong and that she couldn't begin to express how sorry she was for the pain she had caused. She had had Alyssa's best interests at heart, but she had seen for herself what that really meant—staying with Jared.

His gaze found Genna's, and he murmured two words before pulling her into his arms. "It's over."

Ten

Nothing could have prepared Genna for the Hennessy clan. Jared had warned her of their imminent arrival. He had come right out and told her they were totally off the wall. But when they descended en masse the week before Jared was to leave for training camp, Genna was positive Tory Hills would never be the same.

She stood on Jared's front porch, fidgeting. He had insisted she be there when the family arrived. Right off the bat she had thought that wasn't such a hot idea. She had protested, pointing out to him that he should let everyone settle in and relax before trying to make introductions. But trying to get Jared to see reason when he didn't want to was as futile as trying to balance Otis Paige on the head of a pin.

So she stood on the porch with her hands buried in the pockets of her khaki shorts, scuffing up her loafers as she nervously bent her feet over on their sides and back. She wished Bernice hadn't abandoned her to go bowling; it would have been nice to see another familiar face in what she imagined would be a sea of loony Hennessys.

"When are they coming?" Alyssa asked for the millionth time as she tugged at the leg band of her lacy white panties.

"Soon, honey." Genna bent to smooth down the girl's navy and white dress yet again.

"You said that a long time ago," Alyssa said with a scowl.

"Well, it takes a long time to get here from the airport."

"What if they never get here? What if they get lost?"

"They won't get lost. Your dad knows how to get there and back."

"What if he forgets?"

"He won't."

"What if—"

The Dennisons' burgundy van screamed around the corner and slid to a jolting halt in front of Jared's house. All the doors opened at once and people spilled out of it talking a mile a minute. Alyssa bounded off the porch and dashed for the group. Genna remained rooted to the spot in frozen shock. Suddenly a grinning Jared grabbed her by the arm and dragged her into the middle of the crowd to make introductions before anyone even made it to the house.

Bill Hennessy, Jared's father, stood all of five feet nine inches tall and was built like a whip. He had a full head of gray-streaked nut-brown hair which he wore long and slicked back. He was a handsome man. Jared had obviously inherited his father's short straight nose and strong jaw. Clad in old jeans and a loud red Hawaiian shirt, Bill nodded pleasantly through the introduction, never stopped chewing his bubble gum, and immediately wandered off toward the garage jotting down notes in a green steno pad with a felt-tip pen.

"Dad has lots of ideas," Jared explained enthusiastically, swinging Genna toward his mother. He nearly had to shout to be heard above the racket. "Mom. Mom! This is Genna."

Grace Hennessy broke off her conversation with one of the other Hennessys and turned to look down at Genna with eyes so blue they were almost startling. Grace was six feet tall if she was an inch and possessed a magnificent mane of raven-black hair. She wore what could be described only as a "flowing robe," a long, layered, diaphanous caftan in lavender and deep purple. A trio of wide silver bracelets rattled on her arm as she reached out to take Genna's hand. Her smile rivaled the sun for brilliance.

"So you're Genna. Jared told us all about how you helped him through the ugly business with Simone. We all owe you a huge thank-you, darling."

Genna blushed as Grace engulfed her in an exuberant embrace. "I didn't really do all that much," she protested.

Grace ignored her remark and pinned her son with a meaningful stare. "I'm so glad we survived the drive from the airport so we could meet you, Genna."

"Mom," Jared said between his teeth.

Grace pressed onward, undaunted, "Jared couldn't get us here fast enough, could you, Jared?"

Genna shot him a curious glance. He was blushing like a sheepish teenager.

"Now, Mom—"

"And I can see why," Grace continued, a familiar twinkle in her eye as she ignored her sputtering son and gave her full attention back to Genna. "But he really should have gotten a ticket—"

"Mom!"

"He must have scared a year off the lives of those little nuns in the VW."

By now Genna was biting her lip. Grace was giving Jared a little of his own medicine which, Genna thought, he richly deserved. She felt an instant bond with Grace.

"I tried to tell that officer to go ahead and write the ticket, but—"

"You got stopped?" Genna asked, trying hard not to laugh at the fierce look on J.J.'s face. "And no ticket? Just how fast were you going?"

"Not that fast."

"Sixty-five in a forty mile zone," Grace supplied.

Jared scowled at his mother and steered Genna away.

"The trooper was a Hawks fan?" Genna suggested sweetly.

"Meet my aunt Roberta, Genna," he said quickly, his look clearly telling her the previous subject was being dropped. "Aunt Roberta, this is Genna. Genna, my mother's sister, Roberta Palmer."

"Nice to meet you." Genna smiled.

"Oh, my word, J.J.!" Roberta exclaimed in a voice as rough as sandpaper. A cigarette bobbed up and down on her lip. She was a thin, birdlike creature with a bird's nest of gray hair and black brows that winged over glassy green eyes. "She's a *doll*! A doll." Her eyes bore right through Genna. "Oh, honey, you're just a *doll*!"

"Th-thank you," Genna stammered, not quite certain how to react.

"She's a doughnut or two shy of a dozen," Jared whispered, tapping a finger to his temple as he herded Genna toward yet another Hennessy.

There was his elder brother, James, a priest. Alyssa called him "Uncle Father." And youngest sister Marie, who was seventeen and in training to make the Olympic team as a figure skater. Rounding out the group was the youngest brother Bryan, a graduate student of parapsychology at Purdue.

The plan was for the group to stay the week, with more family members arriving on the weekend for Grace's surprise birthday party. Grace and Bill were staying on to take care of Alyssa while Jared was away at training camp.

The bulk of the group disappeared into the house, leaving Jared and Genna standing on the sidewalk.

"So, what do you think?" Jared asked, his expression boyishly expectant.

"Oh . . . they're . . ." Genna felt shell-shocked. Her head bobbed around as if the action might jar loose an appropriate word. "Overwhelming."

"Yeah." He grinned. "They're great, huh?"

"Eeeek!"

A blood-curdling scream prevented further discussion and sent the two of them tearing into the house and up the stairs on the heels of the rest of the family. Aunt Roberta staggered out of the bathroom into the hall, where everyone stood staring at her.

"Oh, mercy, J.J.!" she gasped, clutching his arm. "There's a dead woman in your bathtub? How the hell did she get there?"

All eyes swiveled to Jared, who said, "She's not dead, she's a dummy."

Roberta clucked at him and glanced askance at James. "Don't be disrespectful of the dead, J.J. Not in front of a priest."

Genna peered in the bathroom door. Candy the mannequin sat in the bathtub wearing a red and white striped towel and a polka dot shower cap, a back brush taped in her hand.

"She was out of your sight there," Jared said in answer to Genna's raised eyebrow.

"The back brush is a nice touch," James said.

"She couldn't hold on to the loofah," Jared explained.

Everyone nodded in agreement.

Genna closed her eyes and leaned her forehead against the doorframe.

Half an hour later, when everyone was gathering in the dining room for lunch, Roberta pulled Jared aside.

"J.J., honey, I don't know what you paid for this house, but I think you ought to know there are birds nesting upstairs."

"Birds?" Jared glanced at Genna, who glanced at Roberta and back to Jared.

"Birds. I went into the closet in my room and there they were." She took a long drag on her cigarette and exhaled a stream of blue smoke. "Damn near had a heart attack. Heart attack. You've never seen the like; they're huge and pink."

Genna bit her lip and turned away, the mental image of Aunt Roberta discovering a stand of flamingos in the closet was almost more than she could handle.

Roberta tapped Jared's shoulder. "You'd better get them out of there, honey, or they'll make a hell of a mess."

Life was certainly anything but dull with Jared's family in residence. His house was constantly bustling with activity. Bill was forever busy with his notes and diagrams and trips to the garage that involved some secret project. Bryan had the upstairs of the house booby-trapped with electronic contraptions to detect any paranormal behavior; Aunt Roberta kept setting them off. When Grace wasn't regaling the neighborhood kids with one-woman dramatizations of fairy tales, she was sneaking off to enjoy a secret cigarette (she had supposedly quit smoking two years before). The Hennessy siblings were always involved in some sport in the yard.

They were a diverse and overwhelming group, and Genna felt about as interesting as a wet newspaper when she was around them. She liked Jared's family, but all their unique qualities cast one glaring spotlight on her ordinariness. It had never bothered her that she was an ordinary sort of person. In fact, she had always made an effort to be as ordinary as possible. Now she suddenly found it depressing, and it was doubly depressing because she never had a minute alone with Jared and triply depressing because he didn't seem to care.

On one level Genna understood his desire to be with his family. They lived all over the country, and he didn't often get to see them. But on another level, where new love had only just taken root, she didn't understand at all.

Jared was leaving in a matter of days. In Genna's mind the date of his departure was a deadline. It would mark the end of their summer romance. Jared hadn't said or done anything to make her think differently. They had never spoken of a future together, and the more time she spent with his family, the more convinced she became that they wouldn't have one.

She'd known all along she was no more Jared's type than he was hers. He might like her as a friend and occasional lover, but eventually he would want someone unique, more exciting than a kindergarten teacher and compulsive cook. Maybe that was what he was trying to tell her by insisting she come to dinner every night while his family was there. He was probably hoping she would take the hint and bow out gracefully.

The wonder was that he'd been attracted to her at all. Jared was an attractive, athletic, popular man. She was from the studious, sensible-shoes group. The two didn't mix. It wasn't anything personal, it was just chemistry. She'd known about that since junior high.

She'd been right all along in looking for a man from her own social group. A nice, staid business-type guy wouldn't keep her off balance with his outrageous antics or make her bones turn to cottage cheese with his searing kisses and crushing embraces. There was more to life than raucous fun and unbridled lust. There was constancy, stability, life insurance, golf, and boredom.

All that to look forward to, and she'd spent the whole summer with the wrong man. Well, she was a modern woman, a woman of the eighties. Modern women had affairs like this all the time. They enjoyed men like entrees at a buffet, savoring one then moving on down the table of life to the next without a second thought.

Then why did she feel so miserable?

Because you love him, stupid, and there isn't anything modern about you, she told herself.

Genna simply wasn't capable of giving her love casually. Nor was she capable of sustaining a relationship indefinitely without a commitment.

She wanted something lasting with Jared, but for all her outward appearance of self-assurance, the plain unvarnished truth was that she was scared. She was scared to ask Jared for more, for fear of losing him as a friend. They'd had an understanding going into this relationship; now she wanted to renege on the deal and cling to him like ivy to a brick building.

What would he think of her if he knew that? Simple. He'd feel sorry for her, be embarrassed for her, maybe even be angry. She knew; she'd been through it all before.

It would be better, safer, to just let the flame die out. She would let him go, and she would get over him just as she had promised herself. At least that way she would still have a very good friend and she would still have her pride.

She sat on the edge of Jared's patio with her chin on her drawn-up knees, watching Jared, Marie, Bryan, and Father James play touch football with Jared's Super Bowl game ball. Jared's every move was so unconsciously graceful, it made Genna's breath catch in her throat. His body was one finely tuned human machine. And he had a great fanny too.

The evening was uncomfortably warm. Jared wore nothing but a pair of silky electric blue running shorts and sneakers. When he moved just right, Genna could glimpse the delicious little curve of his muscle where thigh met buttock. The feel of that meaty swell beneath her fingers as they made love was too vivid in her memory, and she had to glance away, catching Grace's watchful eyes on her.

"I suppose a mother shouldn't say so," Grace said airily, "but the boy's got a bod to die for."

Genna smiled. "That's the general consensus."

"Jimmy?" Roberta's black brows bobbed over her glassy eyes. She recrossed her legs and tapped the ash off her cigarette on the arm of her lawn chair. "He's a priest, for heaven's sake, Gracie!"

"Not James. Jared, darling. Though I willingly admit with a mother's pride that all my children are beautiful." Grace held her arms out to Alyssa, her eyes glowing with love. "And my grandchildren. Come sit with Gramma, Alyssa."

Alyssa smiled her shy smile and climbed onto Grace's generous lap, abandoning her game of tug-of-war with Flurry. The puppy ran off with a sock in his mouth.

"My stars, she looks just like you, Gracie. Just like you." Roberta puffed on her cigarette, tapped it on the chair arm again, and looked down at Genna. "Doesn't she look just like Gracie, Jeannine?"

"Yes." Genna didn't bother to correct the slip on her name. Roberta hadn't called her the same thing twice yet. "You do look like your grandma, Lyss."

Alyssa and Grace appeared mutually pleased by that news. Alyssa wrapped the voluminous sleeve of her grandmother's white and lilac gown around her arm.

"You wear such pretty dresses, Gramma."

"You think so?" Grace beamed. "Well, thank you."

"She's got your taste too, Mother," Bill said, blowing a bubble. He sat on the patio to Grace's right, his legs stretched out on the lawn, arms braced behind him for support. He wore ragged cutoffs and a fluorescent-green Hawaiian shirt that made Genna's eyes hurt. His steno pad lay open on his lap, and his felt-tip pen was tucked behind his ear as he watched his children play ball.

"Maybe I'll grow up to be just like you, Gramma," Alyssa speculated.

Grace glowed.

Roberta exhaled a cloud of smoke and reverently crossed herself with her cigarette.

Bill chuckled. "You're in like Flynn now, Lyss."

Alyssa slid off her perch and threw her arms around her grandfather's neck in an exuberant hug. "I love you, Grampa!"

Bill laughed, his pale blue eyes crinkling at the corners just the way Jared's did. He wrapped his arms around his granddaughter and rocked her back and forth. "I love you, too, baby."

Genna tried to choke down the rock in her throat. Jared's family was undeniably weird, but they loved one another and never felt any compunction about showing it. They were forever hugging and kissing and slapping one another on the back. They made Genna's family look like polite strangers. They made her feel like an outsider.

No. That was her own fault. She had always longed to be a part of a family that was secure in loving one another. Spending time with the Hennessys only reminded her that she wasn't, and her prospects weren't so great either. She bit her lip and stroked the puppy, who had fallen asleep on her lap.

An exultant cry of "Touchdown!" from Father James drew her attention to the lawn. James was several years older than Jared, and the guy was drop-dead handsome. Not as handsome as Jared, of course, she hastened to amend, but handsome. In his cutoffs and white polo shirt, his black hair windblown, Genna could easily imagine he'd broken a lot of hearts when he'd taken the vows. And no doubt he heard a lot of confessions about lust.

At the other end of the touchdown pass stood Bryan. Bryan was quiet and studious like his father. He never said more than five words at a crack. He wasn't as tall as his brothers, but he was athletically built. His hair was almost blond, and he wore black-framed glasses over fathomless blue eyes. Women must itch to take those glasses off him.

Marie looked like her father with a Dorothy Hamill hairdo. Jared lifted her over his head and turned around and around as if they were pairs skaters, Marie changing leg positions for dramatic effect, then somersaulting down in front of him.

Jared laughed and jogged over to where Genna sat looking forlorn and forgotten. She had begged out of the football game, claiming her ankle was bothering her, but he had his doubts about that. She'd been getting quieter and quieter all week, and nothing he did to tease her out of her mood worked. He was terrified she was getting ready to back out of their relationship. In two days he would be leaving for training camp, what better time for her to break it off?

Dammit, he thought, grabbing up his discarded T-shirt and toweling himself off with it, things had been going so well. What had triggered this? His family? Genna seemed to genuinely like them, but they were an eccentric bunch, and she wasn't into that. Had being around them sent her back to believing he wasn't her type or some such ridiculous nonsense? That made sense, according to the way Genna's mind worked. He was going to have to find out soon and set her straight on a few things.

He would have to be careful about it, though. He had promised her to keep things light. He couldn't just up and tell her he was changing the rules of the game.

"Hey, gorgeous, how's the ankle?" he asked, dropping down beside her, a teasing grin on his face.

"Fine." She flashed him a smile that she feared fell short of looking authentic.

He reached out and tipped her chin his way, stealing a kiss.

"Don't kiss in front of the priest, J.J.," Roberta scolded, grinding out her cigarette and reaching for the half-empty pack on the white wrought iron table.

Jared laughed. "He's my brother, Aunt Roberta."

"Ha! Don't try to fool me." She shook her cigarette at him. "I can see perfectly well who you're kissing. It's Geneva."

Jared and Grace rolled their eyes. Genna squeezed hers shut. Bill scribbled on his steno pad, then his head shot up and his eyes glazed over.

"Boys," he said, suddenly jumping up and marching for the garage, James, Jared, and Bryan hot on his heels.

"Where do you suppose they're going now, Jemima?" Roberta asked, smoke rolling in a cloud around her head.

"They are undoubtedly in there planning my surprise birthday party," Grace said, fluffing at her hair. It was caught up high on the crown of her head and cascaded dramatically down in a froth of inky ringlets.

"You know about your surprise party?" Genna asked, thinking how disappointed the men would be when they found out.

"Of course."

"Oh, my word, Gracie!" Roberta said between puffs.

"I always know. Bill's given me a surprise party every year for thirty-seven years. Every year I know, and every year he knows I know."

"It's a tradition," Marie said with a mischievous grin that was a female version of Jared's.

Roberta cackled, reaching down to pat Genna's shoulder. "They're a crazy bunch, aren't they, Jeanette?"

When the men emerged from the garage, everyone headed for the house and their nightly game of Trivial Pursuit. Everyone except Genna. She backed away from the door Jared held open.

"I can't stay," she said, sending a vacant smile to the space between James and Jared. She figured they would know she was lying since she was terrible at it, and she had the distinct impression she would burst into tears if she looked into Jared's beautiful eyes.

The brothers exchanged meaningful looks.

"I'll walk you home," Jared said evenly.

They walked across the dew-damp yards, Genna forgetting to limp. Twilight was staining the sky purple and fuchsia in the west. Crickets chirped. Across the street Kyle Dennison and Brad Murray played basketball, the ball thunk-thunking on the Dennisons' driveway.

Jared slipped an arm around Genna's shoulders. He pulled her close to his side and leaned back against her house beside the back door.

"My family driving you crazy?" he asked, only half teasing.

"No," Genna rushed to assure him. "I love your family. They're wonderful."

"Yep. The Weird Wonderful Hennessys they call us back home."

"Your aunt Roberta is priceless."

He laughed fondly. "She's a fruitcake, but she's sweet, isn't she?"

They fell silent for a moment. It was an awkward silence, something they hadn't experienced in their relationship even when Genna had disliked him. The sounds of the evening grew almost unbearably loud around them. A click sounded on Jared's front porch, then a dot of red glowed, indicating Grace had slipped out for one of her secret cigarettes.

Jared turned and braced a hand on either side of Genna's head. "Listen, I know we haven't had any time alone this week. I was thinking maybe later I could slip over for a while and—"

"Not tonight, Jared," she said, shaking her head and lying through her teeth. "This isn't a good week for me."

Damn, he thought, as if they didn't have enough obstacles in their way all of a sudden, now Mother Nature had to get into the act. He brushed Genna's hair back from her face. "We don't have to make love, just be together. We need to talk—"

She shook her head. As badly as she'd craved time alone with Jared this week, her emotions were too raw tonight. She needed to be alone, to build herself up for what she was certain was coming: the end.

"Genna, we need to have a serious talk."

So you can tell me it's over? No thanks.

"Not tonight, Jared. Please. Don't push it, okay?"

Just push off. Right, Genna?

He heaved a sigh and looked away. "Will I see you tomorrow?"

"Um—no—I have some things to do tomorrow."

"Baking for next Easter?" he asked sardonically, stepping back from her.

Sudden tears sprang to Genna's eyes. "What the hell is that supposed to mean?"

"Nothing."

"I thought you were taking your family to New Haven tomorrow anyway. I thought your father wanted to go to the shipyard or something."

"Yeah, well, there's no reason you can't come along. I'd like you to come along."

"I can't."

"Fine."

Another silence fell, this one more awkward than the last. Genna was glad darkness had fallen as well. If she looked as much an emotional wreck as she felt, she didn't want Jared to see her.

"You're coming to Mom's party."

The way he said it made her wonder what he'd do if she refused him. "Yes."

"Good."

Silence.

"So . . ." she started, searching frantically for something to lighten the mood. "What is your dad doing in the garage?"

He flashed a weary version of his famous grin. "He's working on a special fireworks display. He's got a board of sparklers spelling out *Grace* in pink and purple with an exclamation mark that has a built-in rocket launcher that'll shoot up Roman candles."

"Sounds exciting," she said in a tight voice, closer to tears than ever.

The party would be the last she'd see of Jared for weeks, and afterward nothing would be the same. Part of her wanted to spend every minute of every day they had left together wrapped in his arms. But she wouldn't do that. If Jared was ready to let the relationship go, she wasn't going to make a scene. She wasn't going to cling to him and embarrass both of them.

It hurt, but she would tough it out. She was a grown-up. She'd made her own decision to love Jared, knowing what that meant. She'd just have to handle it now.

Jared didn't miss the tension of restrained tears in Genna's voice, or the desperation in his own. "Genna, what's wrong?"

He'd intended to wait until he was sure they would have uninterrupted time to talk about whatever it was that seemed to be pulling her away from him. He'd sworn he wouldn't push her into anything. But the prospect of her tears scrapped his intentions.

Genna gulped back the knot in her throat, wishing Jared hadn't put his hands on her shoulders. She could never think straight when he was this close. "Nothing. Why should anything be wrong?"

"You tell me, honey," he begged, his fingers massaging her tense muscles.

Across the yard Jared's back door slammed and Alyssa called out, "Daddy, are you coming to tuck me in?"

Jared cursed under his breath, then turned and called back to his daughter, "I'll be right home, Lyss."

"You'd better go," Genna whispered, misery welling in her chest so she could barely breathe.

Jared didn't move. He could feel Genna slipping away from him. He wanted to know why. He wanted to stop it from happening.

"Dad-dy!"

"Damn," he muttered. Cupping Genna's face with one hand, he leaned down and kissed her. Her lips were soft and trembled beneath his in a way that made him want to hold her and protect her forever.

"Da-ad-dy!"

"See you at the party," he said. Then he turned and loped off across the grass.

Genna watched him snatch Alyssa up in his arms and disappear into the house. Without turning any lights on, she went inside her own lonely little house, climbed the stairs, and sat on the empty bed, where Jared had made love to her.

Silver moonlight spilled through the open window, lighting the room almost as adequately as a lamp. Genna let her eyes roam over her bedroom, her possessions, and mementos. She had a good life, a fulfilling life. Why did it suddenly seem to stretch before her like a vast wasteland?

Why? That was a good word on a moon-drenched night when she sat alone. Why couldn't Jared Hennessy want her for more than the summer?

A long, soft sigh escaped her as she stretched out on the bed and lay looking out her window at Jared's house. Her eyes were remarkably dry. There was really no sense in crying. Life was life and there wasn't anything she could do about it. She might have been able to change Jared's outward appearance, but she couldn't change what was in his heart—no more than she could change what was in her own.

Eleven

"Hell of a party, isn't it, Jean?" Roberta exhaled a jetstream of blue smoke into the night air. She had borrowed one of Grace's "flowing robes" to wear for the occasion, a chartreuse organdy creation with a kelly green sash. It hung on her like a sack. It made Genna think of the little boys who played shepherds in the Christmas pageant at school, dressed up in their father's bathrobes.

Amy stood on the other side of Jared's aunt. She leaned behind Roberta and gave Genna an incredulous look. Genna cracked the faintest of smiles.

"It's a lovely party, Aunt Roberta. Can I get you a soda or something?"

"Yes, Jenny, yes, you can." She grabbed Genna's hand in an affectionate death grip and stared at her with glassy eyes. "My word, you are *such* a wonderful girl. I just can't tell you. I just can't. Please do get me another soda and put a little 'or something' in it, will you?"

"How much 'or something' has she had?" Amy asked as she and Genna made their way to the long refreshment table set up along the back of the house.

"Probably none. She's a little different."

"Bonkers, you mean."

Amy's gaze raced greedily from one end of the table to the other. Spotlights from the side of the house illuminated the bowls and platters of every size and shape, which were crowded onto the red checkered tablecloth. There was everything from cracked crab to barbecued ribs to fresh strawberries to chocolate cake. Thanks to Genna's donations, there seemed to be an inordinate number of desserts.

Amy grabbed a plate and made one enthusiastic sweep down the table. Genna picked out one stick of celery for herself and mixed a drink for Roberta.

"J.J. sure knows how to throw a party."

"Mmmm," was all Genna had to say, an understatement at the very least.

Brightly colored Chinese lanterns were strung all around the backyard; they even hung around Flurry's White Castle doghouse. Blasting rock music, the traveling stereo system of a Hartford radio station was set up on a flatbed truck parked in the alley. The tuxedoed deejay was dancing on the lawn with Grace, who had outdone herself in a gown of cotton-candy pink with a white feather boa.

As with Jared's first party, the entire neighborhood had been invited. Genna spotted Theron Ralston in his new Willard Scott toupee shoveling shrimp dip onto a paper plate. Theron never passed up free food or a chance to spy on his neighbors. The rotund Mrs. Ralston was trying to eat potato salad and pump information from Bill Hennessy at the same time. Bill went on chewing his bubble gum, making notes in his steno pad, smiling and nodding absently. He had buttoned up the collar of his shocking-blue Hawaiian shirt and worn a thin black necktie for the occasion.

Two more of the Hennessy clan had arrived: Jared's older sister Anne, a sculptor with her mother's taste in clothes, and brother Quinn, an oceanographer. Anne was accompanied by her husband, Armand, and their two children. Quinn had come with his new bride, Kate.

Several of Jared's teammates were present as well. Genna recognized Brutus, the mountain with the mohawk haircut. Dressed in black leather pants and vest, and a black bow tie, he and Aunt Roberta were dancing to a hot tune by the Models. Handsome wide receiver Cory Cooper had captivated Marie's attention.

Neighborhood kids darted through the throng with water pistols. Flurry ran past with a sandal in his mouth. The yard was crowded with people laughing, dancing, singing—in general having a disgustingly good time, Genna thought crossly. She'd gotten almost no sleep the night before and it was definitely showing in her temperament. She was more in the mood for a military coup than one of Jared's parties. And it was all Jared's fault, she had decided in a fit of irrational rationalization. She hadn't wanted to get involved with him in the first place, then he'd gone and made her fall in love with him.

"Lighten up, Gen," Amy said, her voice like metal grating on concrete. "You're in a lousy mood. *Again* I might add."

"Thanks for saying so," Genna said sarcastically, sticking her celery into the patch pocket of her blue and white plaid dirndl skirt. She tossed back a good portion of the drink she'd mixed for Roberta.

"Don't mention it. What's the matter? Is Jared trying to put the flamingos back in the yard?"

"I'll have you know I put them in a closet, Amy," Jared said. He shoved his water pistol into the shoulder holster he wore strapped on over a pastel blue T-shirt that molded to his muscular chest. "I had to move them again, though. They scared the wits out of Aunt Roberta."

"I hope you don't mind my saying so, boss," Bernice said, joining them, "but that wouldn't take much. She's a few numbers shy of bingo, if you know what I mean."

"I know what you mean, Bernice." Jared smiled, resting a hand on the woman's shoulder. "And you can say anything you want as long as you keep me supplied in homemade pasta." He sent a sizzling look Genna's way. "Right, Gen?"

Genna glared at him and polished off the rest of Roberta's rum and Coke.

"Besides, Bernice," Jared went on, "you've got a place with me as long as you keep calling me 'boss.' It builds up my self-esteem."

"Build it up any more and you'll have to push it around in a shopping cart," Genna said sardonically.

Bernice laughed. "You'll never have to worry about getting a big head with Genna around, boss."

Jared's lips twitched threateningly. His eyes crinkled at the corners with barely suppressed merriment as he gazed down at Genna. Her smoky eyes burned a furious warning at him.

"Naw," he drawled, "that's not what I worry about when Genna's around."

She supposed he could have said worse. Just the same, she ground her heel into his foot as she pushed past him, smiling too sweetly. "Excuse me. I promised to get your aunt a drink."

Jared tried to pass a grimace off as a smile. "I think I could use one myself."

Genna wove in and out of the crowd at the refreshment table, absently filling a plate as she went along, trying to lose Jared. He caught up with her at the beverages.

"My, what a healthy appetite you have, Miss Hastings," he commented, raising a brow at the sight of her plate heaped with barbecued chicken.

Genna's brows lowered in annoyance as she mixed a drink for Roberta, not paying any attention to what she was doing. "I happen to like chicken."

"You happen to *be* one. You've been avoiding me all evening."

"What would give you that incredibly stupid idea?"

"Ha!" he said with a laugh, straight white teeth gleaming under the spotlights. "You put on more moves going through that crowd than Walter Payton!"

Genna pouted as she stirred the drink with a glow-in-the-dark swizzle stick. "Who on earth is Walter Payton?"

Jared ground his teeth. "Never mind." He started mixing himself a drink without even looking to see what bottles he was picking up.

"Is that my drink you have there, Jillian?" Roberta rasped. She stood with her arm around Brutus's lean waist. Brutus looked down at them and grinned maniacally, revealing a gold tooth with his initial engraved on it in old English script.

"Yes, it is. Here you go," Genna said, pushing the plastic cup into the woman's hand and taking an involuntary step back toward Jared.

"Spartacus here is going to breathe fire for us later on, aren't you, darling?" Roberta patted the enormous man on the back the way she might pat a faithful Great Dane. Her cigarette dangled from her lip. "Breathe fire. Isn't that something? I think that's really something."

She took a big gulp of her drink. All the color washed out of her face. "Mother Malone! You sure know how to pour a soda, honey!"

Brutus threw his head back and laughed. He sounded like Vincent Price with a gland condition. Carried away by his festive mood, he grabbed a bottle of Bacardi 151 by the throat and poured half a quart into his mouth. Standing in profile to his audience, he used Roberta's lighter, spewing a stream of fire from his mouth that would have done a flamethrower proud.

"I suppose you're going to try to tell me he's a Rhodes scholar," Genna said to Jared as the unlikely couple danced away, laughing.

J.J. shook his head and said on a long sigh, "Naw. . . ."

He took a sip of the drink he'd mixed and choked. His face turned red, his eyes teared up. When he tried to talk he sounded like Marlon Brando in *The Godfather*. "Listen, Gen, you and I have to have a serious talk before I go. There are some things we need to get straightened out between us."

Genna's heart went to her throat. "Um—a—I'd love to, but I—I—"

Boo Boo Paige walked by nodding a greeting. In desperation Genna latched on to his arm. "I promised Otis this dance."

It was a testimony to adrenaline-induced strength when she actually managed to drag the lineman into the crowd.

She had another close brush with destiny after she had danced Boo Boo into the ground. Luckily, Bill Hennessy walked by at just the right moment with that special look in his eyes, and Jared fell into step with the rest of his brothers as they marched toward the garage.

Later he cornered her at the edge of the patio, where she was providing the silent half of a one-sided conversation with Amy.

"J.J., why'd you invite her anyway?" Amy complained, giving Genna a disgusted look. "She's no fun at all."

"Don't worry, Amy, all she needs is a small adjustment to her biological party barometer. It's been off kilter ever since I've known her. Right, Gen?" He looked down at Genna with a smile designed to melt female hearts. She glanced away. Sliding an arm around Genna's waist, he gave Amy the last of his fading grin. "Excuse us, Amy."

"Where are you dragging me? Genna asked in a huff as Jared towed her off the patio. He was half-carrying her, his hand digging into her side. She tried to squirm out of his grasp, but he was oblivious to her efforts.

Jared said nothing to her at all. He'd had it with her coolness. If she wouldn't let him talk to her rationally, he would let his body do the talking. Give him the brush-off, would she? Ha! No woman could be as hot in his arms as Genna was and not care about him. She practically went up in flames when he touched her. And she'd told him she loved him. He had every intention of reminding her of that little fact. She couldn't just use him for the summer and cast him aside!

He pulled her around the corner of the garage, out of sight of the party crowd, and into his arms. His mouth swooped down and captured hers before she could even pucker up. His lips were hard and demanding. It was a kiss that burned with frustration and penned-up need. He didn't ask, he took, his tongue demanding entrance to the warm, sweet sanctuary of her mouth. Helpless to do otherwise, Genna gave him what he wanted and received the heady pleasure of feeling his big body shudder against her.

Jared molded their bodies together with his embrace, his hands chasing shivers down her spine, his fingers splaying over the soft flesh of her bottom. Deliberately he drew her hips to his. Genna gasped, dizzy with the sudden intoxicating pleasure. Through the thin fabric of her blue plaid skirt she could feel him, hard and urgent against the aching softness between her legs.

The uncertainty she felt about her relationship with Jared conveniently vanished from Genna's mind. The future was suddenly nothing more than an abstract concept. Need was real. The overwhelming desire to be held and touched and loved by this man was real. She loved him, wanted him, and she couldn't think of a single reason not to give herself to him right there and then. The sounds of a hundred people partying on the other side of the garage couldn't penetrate the drumbeat of her heart pounding in her ears.

Jared dragged his mouth from Genna's, trailed it down her throat as she arched it for him, then gathered the last of his sanity and pushed himself away from her. Lord, he'd been ready and willing to take her there along the side of the garage, where anyone could have happened across them.

The cool night air heaving in and out of his lungs, he glanced all around them looking for a handy hideout. He wasn't going to give Genna the chance to change her mind. He was going to make love to her until she was putty in his arms, then he was going to tell her exactly how things were going to be between them.

Theron Ralston's potting shed stood on the back corner of the lot next door. In one swift move Jared yanked the door open and pulled Genna inside. Moonlight spilled in through a postage-stamp-sized window, outlining a lawn mower and long-handled garden tools. It also fell on the harsh lines of Jared's determined expression, making Genna's breath catch. All predatory male, he backed her against the corrugated metal wall.

"I want you, Genna," he growled low in his throat. He braced a hand on either side of her head as his thighs brushed hers. "Don't give me any nonsense about not wanting me back."

Eyes wide, she shook her head. Jared had been a gentle lover, a playful lover; now he was demanding. She found the contrast exciting in a way that made her knees weak.

His mouth took hers, hot and hungry. Her camisole top pooled at her waist. His fingers peeled away her strapless bra and eagerly claimed her breasts, his thumbs brushing nipples that were hard and aching from sudden desire and the cool night air. Genna's fingers pulled down the zipper of his gray linen slacks, freeing him. She groaned at the feel of him, velvety and warm in her hand.

Need snapped the reins of control and set spurs to their passion. Each thinking this might be their last chance to touch the other, they clung together desperately. Genna's skirt bunched up around her waist. A wisp of blue silk panties fluttered to the floor. Jared's hands grasped her, lifted, and tilted her hips to the appropriate angle before he plunged into her.

They gasped together. He filled her to bursting. She enclosed him in honeyed warmth. With a mutual groan they began to move together, racing toward fulfillment. Genna's legs wrapped around him, drawing him deeper. Jared rewarded her with harder, faster thrusts until his whole body seemed to explode inside her. A deep sound rumbled in his throat. She called his name and dug her nails into the thick muscles of his back, her climax prolonging their pleasure.

Sanity returned to Jared along with even breathing. He was suddenly terrified Genna would hate him. What had seemed like a great game plan when his hormones were running amuck didn't look so hot now. He'd ravished her in his neighbor's potting shed, for heaven's sake! He waited for her to slap him and start calling him names—all of which he richly deserved, he told himself. Instead, Genna, trying to straighten her clothes, began to giggle uncontrollably. He stared at her, dumbfounded.

"We're in Theron Ralston's potting shed!" she managed between giggles.

Relief flooded through Jared, leaving him as weak and delirious as their wild, hasty lovemaking had. It was funny at that, he realized. A brilliant grin splitting his handsome features, he started chuckling. "Old Theron would go into cardiac arrest if he knew I was in here with the kindergarten teacher!"

They tried to laugh without making a lot of noise, like naughty kids who had yet to get caught at their mischief. Jared lifted Genna's silk panties from the floor with one finger, and they collapsed into another fit of laughter, doubling over and leaning against the wall for support.

"Aw, Genna." He wrapped his arms around her and kissed the tip of her nose. "You're a lot of fun, you know?"

Her smile was like a flower that wilted before his eyes. With only the barest tremor in her voice, she asked, "Is that all I am to you, Jared?"

His expression sobered in a flash. How could she think that? He'd told her he loved her. He'd shown her. He'd wooed her and courted her and introduced her to his parents. He'd done everything but prop—propose. A-ha. He'd done everything but clarify one very important point: Their future.

Damn! He'd taken the wrong approach entirely. He'd been so careful not to push her into anything because of her initial reluctance toward him. Now that he thought about it, he'd gone out of his way to make her think their relationship was casual, so as not to scare her off.

How could he have been so stupid? Genna had been burned badly once by assuming a relationship was going to go further. Naturally she was wary of the same thing happening again. He'd been so sure she was giving him the old heave-ho, it had never occurred to him that Genna might be feeling insecure because summer was over and he was leaving in the morning.

"Oh, Genna," he said with a sigh.

Genna braced herself, mistaking the tender, apologetic look in his eyes for pity. *You've done it again, Genna. You should have known better.*

"We've got to have that talk tonight. I have to leave first thing in the morning."

Even though she'd known it, hearing Jared say he was leaving was a hammer blow to her heart. She'd tried so hard to take a sophisticated attitude toward this whole . . . affair. The word was as bitter as aspirin in her mouth. She didn't have affairs. She fell in love. Which was unfortunate, because it seemed no one ever fell in love back.

"Let's go in—" he started.

A movement outside the window had them both ducking down automatically. Genna's heart lodged in her throat like a chicken bone. Was she going to have insult added to injury and be discovered in the potting shed? She could see it now—Theron Ralston would take one look and flip his Willard Scott wig. Theron was so far to the right on the political spectrum it was a wonder he didn't fall off the planet. If he found the kindergarten teacher in his potting shed with a notorious playboy football star, he'd petition to have them put in stocks on the town common at the very least.

Cautiously she peeked out the tiny window.

"Who is it?" Jared whispered.

She sighed with relief. "Just your mother slipping into the garage to sneak a cigarette."

"Oh," he breathed. Cigarette? In the garage. *"Oh, my God!"*

Jared bolted from the potting shed with Genna right behind him as realization struck them both like a bolt of lightning. He shoved her back from the door, sending her rolling in the grass as he plunged inside after his mother. Grace had just struck the match when her son grabbed her arm and yanked her out the door. They hit the ground, tumbling in a tangle of arms and legs and Grace's voluminous pink gown. Jared came up wearing the white feather boa just as an explosion sounded. In the next second the roof of the garage went off like a Roman candle.

Women screamed. Everyone in the backyard dove for cover except Bill and Aunt Roberta. They stood on the far side of the lawn watching fireworks shoot up into the black sky.

"My land, Bill, those are lovely. Just lovely." Roberta perched a hand on one bony hip and puffed on her cigarette.

Bill frowned at the explosion of color in the sky,

pulled his felt-tip pen out from behind his ear, and made a note in his steno pad: Too much gunpowder.

Thankfully Jared had parked his cars on the street so they wouldn't have any difficulty wheeling the fireworks display out. The Corvette and Mercedes had escaped unscathed. The flamingos Jared had moved out from Aunt Roberta's closet hadn't fared as well. The heat from the fire had reduced them to a grotesque mass of molten pink plastic.

The explosion had scattered debris everywhere. The Ralston's vegetable garden was covered with shingles. Golf balls littered the ground like fallen hailstones. Jared had had ten cases of them stored in the rafters of the garage. A grateful sporting goods company had given them to him as a bonus for doing a commercial for their product. One had rendered the Ralstons' poodle unconscious.

A confused paramedic threw cold water on Mrs. Ralston instead of the dog, soaking her dress, plastering the thin fabric to her enormous bosom. Livid, she grabbed a loaf of French bread from the refreshment table and smacked the young man over the head with it.

The fire department had the flames under control in no time, and the deejay kept the music going as partygoers turned into a clean-up crew. Near the Ralstons' potting shed Father James came up with a pair of blue silk panties.

"Size five." He quirked a brow at his brother.

Jared flushed red, giving James a look caught somewhere between indignant and sheepish. He snagged the lingerie away from his brother and stuffed it into his pants pocket, his eyes searching the crowd for the owner of the garment. But Genna was nowhere to be seen.

Twelve

Once they had the fire under control and it had been established that no one had been injured, Genna slipped away. It was after midnight. Jared had his hands full with the firemen and the disaster area that had been his backyard. She doubted he had noticed her wandering away, and that was just how she wanted it.

In a few hours Jared would be leaving for training camp. Genna didn't want to hang around to watch him go, and she certainly didn't want to have that serious talk he kept insisting on.

It wasn't that she was a coward, she thought as she drove down the empty highway out of Tory Hills and into the country. It was just that she couldn't see the sense in embarrassing the both of them with that "I'm sorry you're more involved than I am" speech. She didn't want Jared to feel obligated to give it, and she wanted to retain some small scrap of pride by not being the one he gave it to.

She parked her car off the road under a white oak by a pasture gate and spent some time trying to make out what kind of animals were sleeping on the next hill. Their dark shapes didn't resemble cows. Horses, she decided. She tried to rub a grass stain off her plaid shirt with a tissue.

It was better to let things end this way. Jared would

be gone for three or four weeks. When he came back she'd be busy with school. She'd pretend she hadn't really fallen in love with him, at least not any more than he had with her. They could still be friends. His friendship was precious to her, she didn't want to lose it. She'd never have to let him know she'd gone and broken her heart into a zillion too-familiar pieces hoping for something that was never to be.

She went and sat on the hood of her car as the sun was coming up and finger-combed the grass out of her hair. Sunrise was her favorite time of day. It was the most peaceful time, when most of the world with its problems was still asleep. At sunrise a person could feel nature all around in soft light and stirring breezes. At sunrise a person could think without the events of the day cluttering the mind. At sunrise a person could be totally alone.

Well—she sniffed back a stray tear—so being alone wasn't the greatest thing today. Some days it was wonderful. She would focus on that. Her life was full and rewarding. She was her own complete person, she didn't need to be part of a matched set like crystal salt and pepper shakers. She was an intelligent, reasonably decent-looking person with a job she loved, a comfortable home, good friends, interests, and talents.

Catch 22, she thought. Having this great life made her want to share it with someone special. Jared. And Alyssa.

She was grateful she had had at least some time with Jared, grateful he had bullied her into spending time with him, or she might never had known what a wonderful guy he was. She might never have looked past the punk hair and the diamond earring and the annoying macho act.

The animals in the pasture began to get up and stretch. Funny-looking horses, Genna thought as she watched them crane long necks this way and that. One stood up in the tall grass in front of her car. It was a llama.

Genna shook her head. Nothing was ever what it appeared to be anymore.

Eventually she drove home, showered, and put on a pair of madras plaid shorts and an oversize T-shirt. For an hour and a half she sat on a stool at her kitchen counter and just stared. For the first time in weeks she couldn't think of anything to bake.

At ten o'clock she walked over to Jared's house to make sure everyone was okay after the wild events of the evening. The Corvette wasn't there, so she was certain Jared had gone. She tried to ignore the sense of loss that knowledge brought her.

"Gilda!" Roberta exclaimed as she opened the door. Her gray hair stuck up in every direction, making her look like an exotic bird. She wore red hightop sneakers and a ratty blue bathrobe. Shaking her head, she took a long drag on her cigarette and pulled Genna into the house. "I am *so* glad you dropped by. Our J.J. was looking all over for you."

"Really," Genna said, trying to blink the smoke out of her eyes. *Tough luck, J.J. You'll just have to save your noble speech for someone else.*

"I won't tell James, honey," Roberta said in a conspiratorial whisper. She stuck her cigarette into her mouth and patted Genna's arm. "Really, though, Georgia, you shouldn't fall for a priest. There's no future in it."

Genna sighed and rubbed at the dull headache settling between her eyes. "I just wanted to make sure everyone was okay after last night."

Roberta threw her hands up in the air. "Dead to the world, the lot of them! Dead to the world. Bill's fireworks just did everyone in. Weren't they lovely, Janet?"

"Yes."

"My word, they were beautiful." She stubbed out her cigarette in an overflowing ashtray that balanced precariously on the edge of Jared's cluttered desk, and promptly lit another.

Genna had hoped someone a tad more lucid than Roberta would be up and around, but she had to give up hope of anyone rescuing her. Slowly she started inching back toward the door. "I should be going—"

"Oh, stay!" Roberta exclaimed. "I was just about to have breakfast. Omelettes—chocolate chip and cheese. It's my specialty."

"I'll bet." Genna forced a smile, hoping she didn't look as green as she suddenly felt. She slipped one leg out the screen door. "Really, I can't stay, Aunt Roberta. Thanks for the offer, though."

"Some other time, then. Say, Glenda, some man stopped by from Alyssa's school to pick up her records. I heard J.J. tell Gracie they were in a manila envelope here on his desk, and I just dug around until I found it and gave it to the fellow. Was that all right? Do you think that was all right?"

Genna tossed a glance at Jared's desk. As usual, it looked as though a bomb had gone off on it. "I'm sure that was fine. It was probably Mr. Adams from the secretary's office." She slipped the rest of her body out the door. "Bye now."

"Bye-bye. Come again!" Roberta said, leaning out the door with her cigarette as Genna started across the lawn. "Oh, wait! Wait, Gardenia!"

Genna stopped and turned around to see Roberta disappear into the house. She came back out waving a piece of paper in one hand.

"J.J. left this for you." She handed the paper to Genna.

It was a check for the second half of her salary and a hastily scrawled note thanking her and saying he'd call. That really said it all, didn't it? Genna's heart sank to a new low. She'd been his for the summer, bought and paid for.

Back in her own house, Genna settled down on a dining room chair prepared to do some heavy staring. She decided she would take it up as a hobby since it was easy, cheap, and portable.

The back door banged.

"You're not baking," Amy said as quietly as her grating voice allowed.

"No. I've covered every major holiday through 1990. I even did Hanukkah and Queen Elizabeth's birthday."

"So, what are you doing?" she asked, planting her plumpness on the chair opposite Genna's.

"I'm staring."

Out of deference for her friend, Amy sat and stared for a minute. She didn't have the required patience to do it well, however.

"Where did you go after all the excitement last night?" she asked, focusing on a deep red apple in a wicker basket on the table.

"I went to watch the sun rise on the llamas."

Amy thought it best to let that one slide. She pretended not to have heard. "J.J. was looking all over for you."

"I wanted to be alone. Explosions do that to me. I just need to go off after a good explosion and be by myself."

"Bull roar." Amy blinked as her eyes teared up. "You ran out of here like Walter Payton."

Genna managed to scowl and stare at the same time. "Who *is* this Walter Payton guy?"

"Never mind," she said. "So did you guys have a fight, or what?"

"What would we have to fight about?"

"Since when do you need a reason? You haven't been rational since he moved in. Maybe you got into a fight about your relationship."

"We don't have a relationship. Not in the sense you mean."

"Genna," Amy barked, abandoning her attempt at staring to glare at Genna, "can the crap. We're best friends, remember?"

Genna broke her staring and held a hand up to halt what was undoubtedly going to be one of Amy's lectures. "I freely admit to being involved with Jared. I freely admit to being in love with Jared. But as far as he's concerned, we're just friends who had a fun summer together."

Amy screwed up her pudgy face and gave an unladylike snort that was a pretty good imitation of a whoopie cushion. "You get the most asinine ideas—"

"It's the truth," Genna said wearily. "We made a deal: We'd have a light summer romance, no strings attached."

"What a bunch of hooey! The guy is in love with you!"

"Yeah? Well . . ." She handed Amy the note Jared had left her. "I'm no authority, but this doesn't win any prize as a love letter in my book."

" 'Genna, thanks for all the good work. I'll call you when I get a chance.' " Amy frowned in confusion. Genna and Jared's relationship may have started out light, but she'd have sworn J.J. had fallen in love at least as much as Genna had. She couldn't have missed the mark by that much. Something here didn't fit, and she was going to find out what. Meanwhile, she'd stall as best she could. She slid the slip of paper back across the table. "This is no kind of evidence. It'd never stand up in court. It doesn't prove anything."

"You've been watching *Divorce Court* again, haven't you?" A long, slow sigh slid out of Genna. For a moment she just sat there doodling storm clouds over sad faces on the back of the note. "I wish you were right, friend. I for one don't have to be hit over the head to get the message.

I just have to get my heart broken.

God would have had no trouble creating the world in seven days, Genna thought, if each of those days had been as long as the ones that followed Jared's departure. In fact, He probably could have taken an extra day off. It seemed to her she counted every second of every minute of every hour of Saturday, Sunday, and Monday. Not crying, not feeling sorry for herself, not feeling anything but empty.

One thing she was sure of, she would never fall in love again. It wasn't because she was bitter or afraid. It was because she'd given all she had. She was just fresh out of love for men—good, bad, or otherwise.

Running on empty, she spent her time on such activities as watching her oven clean itself, and even that was too strenuous.

Monday evening she forced herself to drag out boxes of bulletin board materials that she had accumulated over eight years of teaching, inviting Amy to keep her company and help her sort through the mountains of construction-paper alphabets and animal cutouts. The subject of J.J. Hennessy was immediately declared off limits, at least as far as romance was concerned. They couldn't totally avoid him as a topic, since Alyssa was present. Genna had volunteered to baby-sit while Grace and Bill took Aunt Roberta to the airport.

Alyssa seemed even more subdued than Genna. She sat on the love seat in her nightgown with Dollie, regarding a coloring book with uncharacteristic apathy and paying little or no attention to the Disney movie Genna had rented for her. When bedtime rolled around, the tears began to flow. Jared's daughter was convinced her father was never coming home, just as her mother had never come home after their accident.

Genna didn't hesitate to dial the number Jared had left with his parents in case of emergency, but she had to admit to being reluctant to speak with him. While she was waiting for him to come on the line, she decided she wouldn't give him a chance to start a personal conversation. Alyssa was the only reason she was calling.

"Jared, this is Genna," she said above Alyssa's sobs. The little girl had her head pressed to Genna's shoulder, her tears soaking into Genna's gray T-shirt. "I'm baby-sitting Lyssa and we're having a little problem. She thinks you're not coming home—ever."

Before Jared could say anything, she handed the receiver to Alyssa.

"D-daddy?"

"Hey, muffin, what's wrong?" Jared asked, guilt riding him hard. He had wanted to call his daughter sooner, but there just hadn't been time. He should have made time.

"Are y-you in h-heaven?"

Jared's heart lodged firmly in his throat. "No, baby," he assured hoarsely. "I'm at training camp. They don't have phones in heaven, sweetheart."

"Are you sure?"

"I'm sure." He grimaced as he leaned back against the headboard of his bed. Every muscle in his body felt as if it'd been put through a Veg-O-Matic. "I'm a long way from heaven. I'm at training camp. We talked all about that, remember?"

Jared talked until Alyssa sounded relaxed and was reasonably certain she was going to see him again. He promised to call her every night before her bedtime from now on, then he told her to have sweet dreams and asked to speak to Genna again.

Genna, he thought with a smile, adjusting the ice pack on his shoulder. Already he missed her like crazy. He frowned, though, when she came back on the line because her voice sounded like something fresh out of the freezer.

"That do the trick?" he asked.

"Yes, I'm sure she'll be fine now," Genna said, determined to terminate the conversation posthaste. "Thank you, J.J. Sorry we had to disturb you."

He realized with no small amount of surprise that she was about to hang up, and he rushed to keep her on the line. "Gen, did you get my note?" He'd been on pins and needles wondering how she'd reacted.

The jerk! she thought, shooting the phone a narrow-eyed look of outrage. Did he think she was some kind of half-wit?

"Yes," she snapped. "General Motors and I thank you."

Jared winced at the sound of the receiver slamming down on the other end of the line. What had he done now? He knew he hadn't spent much time composing the note—he'd had to spend too much time trying to track Genna down—but he didn't think it was all that bad. And what did GM have to do with their future? She had to have been referring to his check and the car payments she would make with it. He would have thought a marriage proposal would have ranked above auto financing in Genna's mind. She was probably angry he hadn't called sooner, but the first few days of camp were always hectic for him. He hoped she'd understand that when he explained.

He waited an hour before calling back, to be sure Alyssa was asleep, so they could talk without interruption. He decided it would be best to work up to the subject of his note slowly, given Genna's apparent mood.

"Hi, it's me. Everything under control?"

Genna heaved a sigh and rolled her eyes at Amy, who sat cross-legged on the floor sorting through woolly, cotton-ball sheep. She had never taken Jared for a sadist, but he seemed determined to rub her nose in the end of their relationship. She decided to be incredibly sophisticated about the whole thing and deny any heartbreak he might egotistically believe he'd caused. "Lyssa's sound asleep. So . . . how's summer camp going?"

Jared gave a nervous laugh. His instincts were telling him something was definitely wrong here. He and his lady love seemed to be working out of different playbooks. "That's *training* camp."

"Oh. Sorry. How's it going?"

"It stinks. I hate it."

"Gee, that's too bad," she said without a lick of sincerity.

"It's okay. I always hate it. Everybody does. We've got an assistant coach who thinks he's still in the Marines and a rookie quarterback who thinks he's the next Jim McMahon."

"Is he any relation to Ed McMahon?" she asked with bored indifference, which was not an easy task, given the fact that every muscle in her body was so tight she was trembling and she had a pressure behind her eyes that felt suspiciously like tears.

"No, he's not," Jared said, his heart sinking slowly toward his stomach. She didn't sound like a lady who was making wedding plans. Maybe she wanted a little persuading. "You know, I'm really glad you were there for Lyssa. You're so good with her."

"You're welcome." *This had better not be the "what a good friend you are" speech.*

"You've been an awfully good friend."

One succinct if vulgar word crossed Genna's mind as the tears started to pool in her eyes.

"I think Alyssa sees you as a kind of second mother."

Self-preservation forced her to swallow the lump in her throat and put a stop to this before she dissolved into the pile of debris at her feet. "Look, Jared, I know what you're trying to do, but it isn't necessary."

"It's not?"

"No. I'm perfectly aware the romance has gone out of our relationship."

"It has?" His heart dropped the rest of the way and plopped into his churning stomach. Had he misread the situation again? He had been so sure—

"That was the deal, after all."

"But—" That blasted deal!

"So, it was a fun summer. I don't have any regrets—"

"Genna, honey," he interrupted. Nothing was making sense. It was worse than trying to have a conversation with Aunt Roberta. "You sound upset—"

"Ha!" She laughed hysterically. So much for sophistication. "Why should I sound upset?"

"Ask him about the note!" Amy prompted, poking Genna's jean-clad leg with a cardboard giraffe.

Genna made an angry face and waved her off.

"Well, I don't know!" he said, exasperated, pulling his ice pack from behind his shoulder and settling it firmly on his head. "It seems to have something to do with the note. If you hadn't taken off after the fire, we could've just talked—"

"That's okay," she snarled. "I can read English. I got the message loud and clear. You don't have to beat me over the head with it, Hennessy. It's over! It's over and I wish it'd never ever started!"

For the second time that evening Jared sat back and stared at the phone. He felt ten times worse now than he had after practice, where two rookie defensive ends had tried to break him in two. He was stunned. Genna was through with him. He didn't know how he'd managed to do it, but he'd lost her.

Genna left Amy sputtering in the living room. Ignoring her friend's demands for information, she walked out the back door and dropped onto the lounge chair to stare unseeing up at the stars.

You've blown it royally this time, Hastings. After the way she'd behaved, she'd be lucky if Jared ever spoke to her again. She'd agreed to the terms; she had no right to be angry because he'd stuck to them. Now she'd not only lost her heart, she'd lost her friend as well.

Thirteen

"I wish I'd never let you talk me into this," Genna muttered for the eighty-ninth time as Amy turned her car in at the gate of Hawks-Riverside Stadium.

"Quit your whining," Amy complained. She stopped and showed her pass to the security guard. "You want to patch things up with J.J., right? You still want to be friends, right? So this is the perfect opportunity."

"But he didn't invite me, he invited you," she pointed out yet again. Her fingers fidgeted with the big red bow on the huge box of cookies she'd brought as a peace offering. "I still don't see why Brian didn't come with you. I'd think a reception for his favorite football team would have taken precedence over a Kiwanis meeting."

Amy bypassed the larger parking lots and parked her car near a lower-level entrance, hoping Genna was too frazzled to notice there were only half a dozen other cars in the lot. What she wouldn't go through for her lunkheaded friends, she thought fondly. Genna couldn't see past the nose on her face, and Jared—she shook her head as she dropped her keys in her purse. What would they do without me? she wondered.

"I told you. Tonight is their big meeting about the Founder's Day Feast. The barbecued chicken faction needed his vote."

"I hope they win after last year's disaster. Hash and beets don't rank way up there on the feast list with most people."

Kamikaze butterflies were attacking the walls of her stomach as Genna climbed out of the car. She smoothed down the skirt of her purple taffeta dress. "Are you sure we're not overdressed?"

Amy smiled down at her new black silk slacks and gold lamé tunic she had acquired courtesy of a very grateful J.J. Hennessy. "Not at all. This is a real hoity-toity deal. The owners of the team and all the sponsors and sportswriters and all those big mucky-mucks will be here. They do this every year," she lied. "Don't you ever read the sports section?"

"No," Genna replied as she heaved open the steel door and they stepped into a long hallway with yellow block walls and a plain concrete floor.

Thank heaven, Amy said to herself. If Genna read the sports page, then she would have known the Hawks didn't train at the stadium, but out at their own facility near Newington.

Amy turned right and started down the hall with Genna trailing one reluctant step behind.

"I'm sure he won't be happy to see me," Genna muttered, chewing the lipstick off her lower lip. "He would have called—"

"Will you put a cork in it? How could he call? Your phone has been off the hook for four days. Tell me how he could've called."

They stopped near the darkened runway that led to the playing field. Genna tried to picture the look on Jared's face when he saw her at the reception. She could only hope he wouldn't have the bouncer toss her out. "I think I'm going to be sick."

"I think you're making *me* sick. Will you get a grip on yourself?"

Genna scowled and looked up and down the corridor. There wasn't a soul to be seen. "Are you sure this is the right night?" She shifted from one slim black heel to the other, clutching her cookie box to her chest.

"Maybe we're early," Amy said. "You wait here, I'll see if there's anybody in the locker room who can tell me."

"Amy!" Genna yelled, horrified. "You can't just walk into the locker room. What if there are men in there?"

Amy paused at the door, across the hall, a comic grin on her face. "I should be so lucky."

Genna held her breath and waited for angry shouts to come out of the room, but none came. No one came out either. She leaned back against the concrete block wall, immediately gasping and jerking away from the cold, clammy surface. Goose bumps ran down her bare back. She couldn't decide which was worse—worrying about Jared not wanting to be friends anymore, or thinking about the late movie she'd seen three nights before that had been set in a stadium not unlike this one, where an ax-wielding maniac had chased down and pulverized one plucky cheerleader after another.

One side of her cookie box caved in under the pressure of her hands. What the devil was taking Amy so long?

Suddenly the locker room door swung open and an enormous ghoul loomed over her. She screamed, a bloodcurdling sound that shrieked down the cavernous hallway.

"It's only me, Miss Hastings," rumbled a deep bass voice.

"Brutus!" Genna braced a hand against the wall to hold herself up. Her whole body felt as if it were made of fresh taffy, her heart pounded against her ribs like a paddle ball, and she gasped for enough oxygen to keep from fainting. "You startled me."

She worked her facial muscles into what she hoped was a smile and looked up at him. He had gold glitter in his mohawk and wore a big gold hoop earring. Ghoul or Brutus—was there a whole heck of a lot of difference?

"Sorry," he said with a distinctly unapologetic smile. His gold tooth gleamed dully in the light of the hall.

The fact that he was wearing a tuxedo slowly penetrated Genna's brain. A real tuxedo, with a shirt and everything. There wasn't a scrap of leather on him. "My, you're very handsomely turned out this evening. For the big reception, I suppose?"

He made a sound in his throat that was close to a panther's purring. He offered Genna his arm. "This way, please."

Who in their right mind would refuse him? she wondered. As he led the way toward the entrance to the field, she glanced back nervously toward the locker room. "My friend Amy—did you happen to see her in there?"

"Mmmmmmmm . . ." he purred.

Genna gulped.

As they stepped onto the playing field, lights came on just above the lower deck of seats. Not the bright lights the team played night games under, but more like security lights. They were just enough to illuminate the artificial turf with a hazy glow. At center field stood a table set for two, draped in fine white linen. As they drew closer to it, Genna could see the gleam of china and silver, the sparkle of crystal. A dozen white tapers burned in sterling candelabra. Across from it, delicate pink tiger lilies were displayed in a Waterford vase.

Genna was too stunned to think, much less speak, as Brutus seated her at the table. She sat back and listened to the stadium organist playing a mellow, romanticized version of "Lady of Spain." Brutus retreated with her cookie box to the sideline, where he stationed himself like a monolith.

Otis appeared in a tux with a lavender bow tie. He filled her champagne glass and the one at the setting opposite her. Still, Genna said nothing. She was too dumbfounded even to speculate. One thing was certain, this party wasn't set up for a bevy of bigwigs. It was strictly a pairs event—one pair, and she was half of it.

"Your waiter's name is Stephan," Otis said in a well-modulated voice. "The main course this evening is fondue Bourguignonne."

"And here I thought a hot dog was the best you could do at the ballpark," Genna said with a weak laugh.

Otis merely smiled politely. "May I direct your attention to our scoreboard, Miss Hastings?"

The ultramodern electronic board came to life in a blaze of lights.

WELCOME TO HAWKS-RIVERSIDE STADIUM

HOME OF THE WORLD CHAMPION HARTFORD
HAWKS!!!

The organist interrupted his song with a brief rendition of Charge!

TONIGHT'S CONTEST: HASTINGS VS. HENNESSY
GO HAWKS GO! GO HAWKS GO! GO HAWKS GO!
GO HAWKS GO!

A BIG HAWKS-FAN WELCOME FOR LEAGUE MVP
J. J. HENNESSY!!!

The last sentence was punctuated by several bars of an Irish jig from the organist, who then promptly segued into a tango.

Genna put a hand to her mouth to stifle her giggles as J.J. approached from the other end of the field. She still didn't know what was going on, but she no longer felt apprehensive. Jared couldn't have been too angry with her to have arranged such an elaborate affair.

She couldn't believe how good it was to see him. He hadn't been gone a week, but she'd been afraid the only time she would see him up close again was at parent-teacher conferences. Even his wild getup looked good to Genna. He wore a black fedora pulled low over his eyes and a very trendy Italian-cut silver-gray suit, over which he wore a long coat of billowing white parachute silk. As he neared her, she could see his diamond earring glittering under the lights.

J.J. felt as if he had a live hamster in his stomach as he walked across the field. What if Amy were wrong? What if Genna really was through with him? Just because she didn't know about his proposal didn't mean she'd say yes when she found out. She'd probably call him an uncouth boor and dump the ice bucket over his head.

She looked like a million bucks in that dress. He'd been so miserable missing her, he'd been driving his teammates nuts. Several of them had suggested he take a soak in the whirlpool—headfirst. If she didn't want him—

Before he could turn tail and run, Brutus appeared beside him to take his coat and hat, and then returned to the sidelines.

"Hi, gorgeous," Jared said in a voice like dark velvet as he slid onto the chair across from Genna.

"Hi," she said with a tremulous smile. She gestured to the stadium in general, the elaborately laid table in particular. "How did you manage all this?"

"Bribery." He grinned.

Her smiled faded away. "What for?"

"Peace offering. An apology dinner."

Genna sat back, tearing her gaze away from the hypnotic blue of his eyes. "I'm the one who should apologize, Jared. I had no right to blow up at you the other night. I got too involved when I knew I shouldn't have, and . . . well . . . I set myself up for it, and heaven knows I can take it on the chin with the best of them. I was just feeling sorry for myself and I took it out on you. If you can forgive me, I'd still like us to be friends."

Speech ended, she tried to clear the tears out of her throat without sounding like a longshoreman. She kept her watery eyes trained on the delicate rose pattern that edged the china.

A little more sure of herself than he had been, Jared leaned across the table, hooking a finger under Genna's stubborn little chin and tipping her face up so he could see into her eyes. "We had a little misunderstanding—"

"I know."

"About the note I left."

"Could we just drop it, J.J.?" she asked, trying not to sound annoyed. Why did he have to go on beating that poor dead horse?

"You missed page two," he said, sitting back in his chair. While she squinted at him suspiciously, he took a fortifying sip of champagne.

"There was no page two," Genna said flatly.

"Yes, there was." It had never occurred to him she wouldn't believe him.

"Why are you doing this to me, Jared? I apologized, what more do you want?"

"Page two—and I quote—" he said. " 'Then we can

make plans to go looking for an engagement ring. I love you. Jared.' "

As he might have predicted, she was speechless. For all of two seconds.

"Baloney!" Genna said, ignoring the part of her that wanted to believe him. If he'd wanted to marry her, he'd have said so. He'd had plenty of opportunity. "There was no page two. What kind of sick joke is this, Hennessy?"

"Joke?" Jared roared indignantly.

"I can tell you right now, it's about as funny as a nuclear holocaust," she said furiously, her eyes scanning the cutlery for a good weapon.

"Look, I like a good joke as much as the next guy, but I'm not about to rent a whole football stadium to play one in. I'm telling you there was a page two!"

"There was not!"

"I ought to know, I wrote it!"

"You ought to have your head examined! There was no page two and this is *not* funny!"

His eyes round and incredulous, Jared raised his hands in a gesture of defeat. Women! "Genna, I want to marry you. Why would I make this up?"

"Because . . ." Abruptly the fight drained out of her. She remembered how Jared had stuck up for her with Allan, how appreciative he'd been of her help with Alyssa and Simone. She remembered what she'd taken for pity in his eyes that night in the potting shed. She twisted her pink linen napkin in her hands, then swiped at the tears that suddenly clung to her lashes. "You're so sweet. You'd do that kind of thing out of some sense of obligation, like that business with your T-shirts. I got in over my head, and you think you have to stick with me because we're a team and all that—"

"Genna, honey," Jared interrupted gently as a sudden thought occurred to him. He covered her hand with one of his, "you're behaving very irrationally lately. Are you pregnant, sweetheart?"

Genna's head came up as all the color washed out of her face and a wave of nausea hit her. It seemed fate had an exceedingly poor sense of humor. Allan hadn't wanted to marry her because she *had been* pregnant, now Jared wanted to marry her only because he thought she *was* pregnant.

She stared at him for what seemed like an hour, hurting in ways she had never even dreamed were possible.

"No, Jared," she said in a deadly whisper, pulling her hand out from under his and sliding her chair back. "You can breathe easy. I'm not going to trap you into anything."

She rose with the dignity of a queen, then turned and bolted for the exit, tears of pain and anger stinging her eyes. Her short legs on high heels were no match for one of the top running quarterbacks in the league, however. While he cursed himself for being ten kinds of a fool, Jared's long legs ate up the yards of turf until he was no longer behind her, but blocking her path. He grabbed her by the shoulders and held firm when she struggled.

"Let me go, Hennessy!" she yelled, resorting to kicking at his shins. He dodged her feet and managed to haul her against him so she couldn't move enough to wound him.

"Genna, honey, I swear on a stack of Bibles that thought came to me just now. It had nothing to do with my proposal—not with the one I just made or the one I left you on Saturday. Ouch!"

He let go of her and grabbed his side where she'd pinched him. Genna backed away, glaring at him. "Drop the phony-note business. I'd throw myself in a shark tank before I'd let you marry me out of some noble sense of duty."

"And I'd jump in ahead of you before I'd offer to do that, Genna," he said, looking as serious as she'd seen him. "I made that mistake once. I wouldn't do it twice. There's only one reason I want to get married again. It's because I love you."

He chanced a step closer, then another. One hand seemed to reach out of its own accord to touch her cheek. She seemed tiny and fragile, her smoky eyes wide and full of uncertainty. Jared thought his heart would burst with love for her, his Genna, who seemed so practical and capable on the outside but was so vulnerable on the inside. He wanted her in his arms, safe forever.

"You really believe we just had a summer fling. You think it's all over between us, don't you?"

"Isn't it?" she asked, her heart in her throat. She didn't dare let herself hope. If she had let herself hope, then she really would be lost when she found out she'd been right all along.

Once again Jared's hand lifted to touch the peachy softness of her cheek. What if she listened to all his arguments and still said no? His heart thudded in his chest like a faulty fuel pump. When he spoke, his voice was that whiskey-on-the-rocks rasp that made Genna's pulse race. "Not if you don't want it to be."

Genna tried to force herself to breathe normally, but it seemed she'd forgotten how. What if he were just being a gentleman and giving her a chance to decline first? She'd been so sure he'd wanted nothing more than the summer. But what if she were wrong?

"I love you," he whispered. "I only said that stuff about us being a summer thing so I wouldn't scare you off. I was afraid to pressure you. You hardly even liked me at the time. I thought if I told you we'd keep it light, you'd give me a chance to prove I wasn't the jerk you thought I was."

Her look was skeptical. He gave her his roguish grin, the Jack Nicholson grin that made Genna's knees sway threateningly. He rested his big hands on her shoulders, repeating his claim with heart-stealing tenderness. "I love you. I told you that."

Genna trembled. She'd heard those words before, and they hadn't meant what she had hoped. They hadn't meant anything. "You told me that in bed, but—"

"But nothing," he said, his expression uncompromising. "When I told you I loved you, I meant it. For all time, not just when you're all warm and soft beneath me."

"Ja-red!" She blushed to the roots of her hair and cast a furtive glance back at Otis and Brutus, who were nearly fifty yards away, sitting on a bench studying their playbooks.

Chuckling, Jared slipped his arms around her waist and started to cuddle and kiss her, attacking her throat with tiny nips and licks. "So, how about it, Teach? Will you marry me?"

"I don't know," Genna said soberly, for once immune to his touch. "I can't get away from the feeling that it's not what you really want. I know I've been a basket case the last few days, and I can see Amy's fine hand in all this." She waved a hand at the empty stadium. "I wouldn't put it past her to have pleaded my case until you broke down and offered to marry me."

J.J. let a smile tease his lips. He brushed a wild lock of chestnut hair from her eyes. "Hey, I'm a great guy, but I wouldn't go as far as marrying someone just to make them feel better.

"Genna, you ought to know by now, I don't play by other people's rules. I wouldn't have asked you if I didn't mean it with all my heart. I don't do anything I don't want to—"

"What about becoming normal?" Genna asked warily.

He made a face. "That was mostly a way to get you to spend time with me. It seemed like a great way to kill two birds with one stone."

Genna gaped at him, furious, and at the same time aware of an undeniable joy flooding through her. "You tricked me!"

"Sort of." He grinned, his eyes alight with mischief. "You wouldn't have had anything to do with me otherwise. I'm not your type, remember, Miss Tunnel Vision? You'd still be looking for a Hart Schaffner and Marx mannequin if not for my brilliant strategy."

"I should bean you for your boneheaded strategy!" She pinched him on the arm and wriggled out of his grasp. "You're a filthy sneak, Hennessy!"

"Ouch!" He rubbed his arm and leered at her teasingly. "I love it when you get abusive, Gen. Do it some more."

"And you're perverted too." She danced away from him. He pursued. She wheeled to face him. They both dodged one way, then the other. Genna turned to retreat, and Jared caught her from behind with his arm around her waist, hauling her back against him. His lips nuzzled the sensitive spot beneath her ear as she wriggled against him in a way that encouraged his hands to wander.

"You're a strange man, Hennessy."

"Yeah," he drawled, sighing into her ear, "but you love me for it . . . don't you?"

She slanted a look at him over her shoulder, her heart swelling at the vulnerability in his eyes. "I guess." She smiled softly. "I guess I love you so much it scares me."

He grinned and resumed nuzzling. "So you'll marry me?"

"I didn't say that."

"Aw, come on, Gen," he pleaded, turning her to face him. "I love you. Alyssa loves you. My family loves you. My dog loves you. My brother's a priest; we'll get a discount on the ceremony."

She frowned at him, but her heart was racing fast enough to break the land speed record. "Was there really a page two?"

Jared took her hand in his and raised it to his chest, tracing an X with her fingers over the silk of his shirt. "Cross my heart."

She pressed her palm flat, feeling the strong, regular rhythm of his heartbeat. Her eyes locked on his. "So where is it?"

"Beats me. I left it on my desk with page one and your check."

"Finally something makes sense! That desk of yours should be declared a national disaster area."

"I promise to clean it if you say yes."

"You'll probably find Jimmy Hoffa," she said dryly.

"I'll set fire to it as soon as I find that blasted page."

Genna grinned. "Maybe we could get your dad to blow it up."

He laughed, relief washing over him. She was going to say yes; he could feel it. He'd find that confounded note, have it framed, and give it to Genna for a wedding gift.

"You actually proposed to me on a piece of scrap paper?" she asked, looking less than pleased with him.

Jared had the grace to look sheepish.

"What a lousy proposal, Hennessy."

"It seemed like a good idea at the time. In retrospect, it stinks. You should have heard what Amy had to say about it." He winced in remembrance as he traced one finger along the delicate V of Genna's collarbone. "My ears are still ringing. She said I'd better come up with something pretty good to make it up to you."

Genna's eyes landed on the table at center field and the waiter who had wheeled out a tray with covered dishes on it. Her gaze found Jared's, and she smiled. "This is pretty special."

"You ain't seen nothin' yet," he said with a grin. He took a step away from her and waved up at a set of windows on the second deck. The scoreboard came to life again as the organist played "Let Me Call You Sweetheart." Cartoon brides and grooms marched across the enormous lighted board, then disappeared.

GENNA, I LOVE YOU MORE THAN A SUNDAY WITH
NO INTERCEPTIONS
I LOVE YOU MORE THAN A WIN AT THE SUPER BOWL
I LOVE YOU MORE THAN ROOT BEER
I LOVE YOU

A little football player ran across the screen, stopping in the center and giving an exaggerated shrug. The next line chased him away.

WILL YOU MARRY ME?
WILL YOU BE MY TEAMMATE FOR THE GAME OF
LIFE?
SAY YES! SAY YES! SAY YES! SAY YES! SAY YES!
SAY YES!

Genna pressed her hands to her cheeks. Tears shimmered in her eyes. She took in the entire scene: the stadium, the table, Stephan the waiter, Otis and Brutus, the scoreboard, the corny sound of the organ. Jared, wearing his heart on his sleeve. He'd gone to a lot of trouble and she'd love him for it until the day she died.

Jared's sexy smile teased his mouth as he looked down at her. His blue eyes glittered like jewels. The stadium lights turned his diamond earring into a prism of brilliant colors. "I feel it only fair to warn you, I'm going to run that at every home game until you say yes."

She laughed out loud and let him take her in his arms, her fingers sliding up the lapels of his suit jacket to tease the back of his neck.

"Gen-na," he singsonged. "Come on, say you'll marry me."

Genna fought a losing battle to keep a straight face.

He was incorrigible. And irresistible. And she loved every molecule of him even if he was a madman. She gave him a lopsided smile. "I guess I'll have to. We're a team. Team players stick together, right?"

"Right." He grinned.

"And we're pretty good together, right?"

With a loving smile Jared lowered his head to touch the tip of his nose to the tip of Genna's nose. "Unbeatable."

"The best."

THE EDITOR'S CORNER

*** PREMIERING NEXT MONTH ***
*** THE HOMETOWN HUNK CONTEST ***
SEE NEXT MONTH'S EDITOR'S CORNER
FOR ENTRY BLANKS

June is certainly a month for gorgeous, passionate, independent, loving, tender, daring, remarkable heroines! With three of the six women of the month being redheads, you can be sure to expect fireworks! Magdelena is washed right into her lover's arms in the rapids; Lux falls into her lover's arms with a giant teddy bear; Meghan has risky plans for her man; Candace finally wants to give all; Lacey's free spirit needs taming; and Randy learns to surrender . . . All this and a whole lot more in our June LOVESWEPTs. Read on to learn about each book and the wonderful heroes who fall in love with these six fabulous heroines.

In **CONFLICT OF INTEREST** by Margie McDonnell, LOVESWEPT #258, Magdelena Dailey, our heroine with long, wild hair, is rescued from a Colorado river by Joshua Wade who steals a passionate kiss as his reward. Joshua is a sweet seducer, a man made for love. Magdelena needs quite a bit of convincing before she changes her plans and lets a man into her life again, and Joshua is up to the challenge. There's no resisting his strong arms and tender smile, and soon Magdelena is riding the rapids of love!

Lux Sherwood is a raven-haired beauty in **WARM FUZZIES,** LOVESWEPT #259, by one of our perennial favorites, Joan Elliott Pickart. All Lux needs is one of her very own creations—a giant teddy bear—to get Patrick "Acer" Mullaney's attention. Acer is a star quarterback with a serious injury that's keeping him out of the game—the game of football, that is. He's definitely strong enough to participate in the game of love, and here's just a taste of what Acer has to say to Lux:

> "My needs run in a different direction. I need to kiss you, hold you, touch you. I need to make love to you until I'm too exhausted to move. I don't want to be just your friend, Lux. I won't be."

(continued)

What's a woman to say to such a declaration? Lux finds the right words, and the right actions in **WARM FUZZIES**!

We're so pleased to bring you our next LOVESWEPT for the month, **DIVINE DESIGN,** #260, by first novelist Mary Kay McComas. With a redheaded heroine like Meghan Shay and her daring scheme, we're certain that Mary Kay McComas is headed for LOVESWEPT success! Her hero in **DIVINE DESIGN** isn't bad either! Who can resist a long, tall Texan whose eyes gleam with intelligence *and* naked desire. Michael Ramsey has all the qualifications that Meghan is looking for—in fact he's too perfect, too good looking, too kind, too wonderful—and she can't help but fall in love, and that's not part of Meghan's plans. Ah, the best laid plans . . .

Barbara Boswell delivers another moving love story with **BABY, BABY,** LOVESWEPT #261. By popular demand, Barbara brings you Candace "Barracuda" Flynn's love story. And what a love story it is! Candace wants a second chance with Nick Torcia, but Nick is wary—as well he should be. Candace burned him once, and he isn't coming back for more. But something has changed. Precious new babies have brought them both an understanding of love. Still, Nick needs to lay the past to rest. Here's a sample of the intensity of their encounter:

> "Why did you lead me on, Candy?" Nick demanded, his onyx eyes burning into hers.
>
> "Not for revenge," she whispered.
>
> "Then why, Candy?"
>
> Her heart seemed to stop beating. He was so close to her, close enough for her to feel the heat emanating from his hard, masculine frame.
>
> "Nick." His name escaped from her throat in a husky whisper, and she tried to move closer. Desire, sharp as a stiletto, sliced through her. She wanted to lose herself in his arms, to feel his hot, hard mouth take hers. She gazed at him with undisguised yearning.
>
> But Nick wouldn't let her close the gap between them. He held her wrists, controlling her movements and keeping her anchored in place. "Tell me, Candy."

Tyler Winter is the man who tames Lacey Lee Wilcox's free spirit in **FOR THE LOVE OF LACEY,** LOVESWEPT #262, by Sandra Chastain. Tyler is a renaissance man—an artist, businessman, and an absolutely irresistible hunk! Is

(continued)

he a flirt or really a man Lacey can trust her heart to? Tyler showers her with kisses, gives her wildflowers, and takes her on picnics, but still Lacey is afraid of losing her heart. With just a little more convincing our heroine loses her fears and listens to her heart:

"Tyler, turn me loose," Lacey ordered.

"Nope," he said, moving his mouth toward hers.

Not again, she begged silently. Too late. She was being kissed, thoroughly kissed, and there was no way to stop him. Tyler finally drew back and grinned down at her with undisguised joy.

"Tyler," she protested, "you don't know what you're doing."

"You're right, and it's been a long time since ignorance felt so good. Kiss me, Lacey."

In **HAWK O'TOOLE'S HOSTAGE** by Sandra Brown, LOVESWEPT #263, Randy Price can't believe what's happening to her. It's 1987, yet she's just been abducted by a masked man on a horse! No, this is not part of the old west show she was watching with her son. Who is this masked man? And why does he want Randy? Hawk O'Toole is an Indian Chief with very good and honorable reasons for kidnapping Randy Price, but he doesn't plan on the intense attraction he feels toward her. She's his hostage, but fate turns the tables, and he becomes her slave. Love has a way of quieting the fiercest battles as Randy and Hawk find out.

Happy Reading! Remember to look for The Hometown Hunk Contest next month—it's your big chance to find the perfect LOVESWEPT hero!

Sincerely,

Kate Hartson

Kate Hartson
Editor
LOVESWEPT
Bantam Books.
666 Fifth Avenue
New York, NY 10103